THE FOOLISH HEART

Mary Bradbourne's aunt brought her up after her parents died. When she was ten, her aunt had a son, Jackie, who was left with a mental disability as the result of an accident. Unselfish and affectionate, Mary dedicated her life to caring for him. But when she meets Dr. Paul Deal and falls in love with him she faces a dilemma. How will she be able to care for her cousin, when she knows she must follow her heart?

PATRICIA ROBINS

THE
FOOLISH
HEART

Complete and Unabridged

LINFORD
Leicester

First published in Great Britain in 1956

First Linford Edition
published 2006

British Library CIP Data

Robins, Patricia, *1921 –*
    The foolish heart.—Large print ed.—
Linford romance library
    1. Love stories fiction
    2. Large type books
    I. Title
    823.9′14 [F]

20170770

ISBN 1–84617–532–1

Published by F
F. A. Thorpe (Publishing)
Anstey, Leicestershire

Set by Words & Graphics Ltd.
Anstey, Leicestershire
Printed and bound in Great Britain by
T. J. International Ltd., Padstow, Cornwall

This book is printed on acid-free paper

For
BETTY HENRY
in affectionate friendship

1

Jackie was feeling better. He sat up in bed, pillows heaped behind him, looking at some brightly coloured picture books. When Mary came in with his cup of mid-morning Ovaltine, he looked up and gave her his bright child-like smile and waved his hands at her.

Mary smiled back at him.

'You've got some colour in your cheeks today, Jackie. The doctor will be pleased when he comes. Now drink up your Ovaltine and then I'll straighten the bed and make you nice and tidy.'

She started to pick up the scraps of paper he had been cutting and put them in the waste-paper basket. She was not unaware of the fact that her own cheeks were glowing and her eyes suspiciously bright, nor that the new young doctor who had been calling to

1

see Jackie during his bout of 'flu was the cause.

Her radiance gave her customary pale rather ethereal prettiness, a real beauty. Most people thought her enormous brown eyes too large for the thin, pointed face and the dead white of her skin and extraordinary almost white-blonde hair. 'Very odd!' they had said to her Aunt. 'Yet one cannot call her plain either. There is something striking about the girl . . . such a queer combination of fair hair and dark eyes.'

Her colouring had come from her Norwegian mother, her dark eyes from her father. Mary knew this, although she could not remember her parents who had both died before she was three. Her father's young sister, Aunt Ethel, had looked after her ever since and she and her husband, Uncle Tom, had been the only 'parents' she had ever known.

Mary never ceased to be aware of the enormous debt she owed to them both. Her parents had left no money and she had had everything a young girl could want from her Aunt. Admittedly Uncle Tom was rich and could well afford to be generous to her, but even when Jackie was born, their adored only child, they had made no difference between their son and their niece.

Mary was ten when the baby was born . . . old enough to understand the great miracle of his birth, and old enough to be thrilled by the thought of a real live 'doll' for her to nurse and hold and help Aunt Ethel and the young nurse to care for. Old enough, too, to be deeply and terribly shocked when the girl fell downstairs while carrying the baby, and to be told by her Aunt a while later that the little boy baby was, as a result of this accident, mentally abnormal. At first she had refused to believe it when her Aunt told her the truth.

'But he's perfect . . . quite the most perfect baby in the whole world!' she had cried, staring aghast at her Aunt's white, stricken face. 'It isn't true!'

But it was, and as the baby grew into a toddler and still could not lift his head from the cot, Mary saw for herself that little Jackie was not normal. When at last she accepted this fact, she simultaneously rejected it. If Jackie was backward, so were lots of other babies. She would spend the rest of her life helping him, encouraging him, making him through her own efforts and determination as much like other children as he could be.

The young nurse had been dismissed and not replaced. With tireless patience, Mary spent all her holidays and any free time she had from school, coaxing the baby to take an interest in the toy she dangled before him . . . to stretch out his hands for it . . . at long last to raise himself a little in an effort to grasp it. He was nearly two when this great triumphant step was taken.

Flushed and bright-eyed, she tore downstairs to her Aunt and Uncle.

'He moved himself . . . Jackie moved!' she cried.

They rushed back upstairs together but the little boy made no further efforts, and only half-believing the radiant little girl's story, her Aunt and Uncle left the nursery.

But Mary had not been mistaken. Gradually, Jackie made further efforts and because it was plain for all to see that he adored Mary, it was always for her that he exerted himself and seemed to be trying his best to please.

Mary did not learn till she was older, the hopeless trek her Aunt made from doctor to doctor, specialist to specialist. None could give her any hope . . . none believed that an operation could be performed to correct his brain.

'He may learn to walk . . . talk . . . eat by himself . . . but you must not count on anything more. His mental age can never exceed that of a child of four or five . . . '

The old doctor who had attended them since they moved to this new district after the tragedy said that

Mary's tireless patience and strong-willed determination were just what Jackie needed and that her faith and her prayers were doing him more good than he, a mere doctor, could do himself.

So Mary grew up, her life punctuated by Jackie's simple achievements. On his bad days, when he would fret and cry, her own little world would be downcast, sad, depressed, even while she crooned her childish songs to him and tried to jolly him out of his moods. The days he first crawled, took his first steps, spoke his first word which was her name, were days she would remember all her life.

Now Mary was twenty and Jackie was as the doctors had said he would be at best . . . a strong, still beautiful little boy of ten but with the mind of a five-year-old child. Mary had known for some time that there could be no improvement, but even while she had accepted this, she had never despaired. Since she had left school, she had appointed herself a kind of governess-companion to the little boy and was constantly teaching him new things which, though he might forget them again as he so often did, at least gave her a feeling that he was progressing. It was the only thing in the world that really counted with her. She had dedicated herself when she was still so young that she had never allowed herself to consider a career as other girls at school did. Her teachers had told her . . . and her Aunt, that she had an excellent brain and might, if she would only concentrate more and apply herself, win a scholarship to University. But even while she had been pleased at the thought that she could have done it had she wished, she agreed with her Aunt who, when they talked it over, said that she would have to live away from home and that Jackie would be miserable without her.

'He loves you so much more than anyone else, Mary, more even than me, his mother. I don't mind that . . . I only mind that it is you he depends on. One day you will want to get married and leave us whereas I, his mother, would stay with him always. I'd never fail him.'

'But you know I will never fail him either!' Mary cried, deeply distressed. 'Jackie means everything in the world to me, too. I'll never marry . . . never.'

'Are you so sure?' her Aunt asked, a curious expression in her eyes. 'You're young and pretty, Mary, and one day you'll fall in love. Jackie won't mean anything then! You'll want . . . I suppose you've every right to expect, that you'll have a home, a husband and children of your own.'

Her voice was bitter and strangely taut.

'I'll never leave Jackie, never!' Mary vowed again from the depth of her sixteen-year-old heart. 'Don't doubt me, Aunt Ethel. Even if I did not love Jackie so much, I'd want to stay for your sake. You and Uncle Tom have been so marvellous to me. I can never repay you for all you've done.'

Her Aunt was white-faced and it seemed to Mary as if a terrible conflict were going on inside her . . . as if she were being torn apart. At last she said in a strangled voice which was barely audible:

'We owe you a lot, too, Mary. You've always been so wonderful to Jackie.'

Mary could not properly conceive the dreadful agony of mind that was her Aunt's constant companion. It seemed to the older woman that at every turn now, she was torn between love for her helpless child and her duty to her niece. Oh, it had been easy enough to be generous and kind to the little girl for those first few years. She and Tom had no children of their own and they had grown deeply genuinely attached to their little niece. She had such a warm, loving disposition that no one who met her could help loving her. But the real depths of her own maternal love were not revealed until her little son was born . . . a love made all the more desperate by the protective quality which was fiercely and primitively to the fore when she realized how helpless

and dependent her child must always
be ... how her friends pitied her
... and Jackie ... and Tom.

Now, suddenly, she was having to
face the worst of all choices. She had
allowed Mary to give her childish love,
interest and attention to Jackie because
the girl had volunteered them from the
start and because daily it became more
and more obvious that Jackie really only
loved and responded to his cousin.
When he was in his trying moods, on
the bad days, he did not even want his
mother near him. Now, too late, she
saw the folly of allowing this tremendous dependence and affection to take
hold of her son. She had not stopped to
think in time that Mary would grow up,
fall in love, and LEAVE JACKIE.

When Mary was sixteen, her Aunt
saw with a fear far exceeding her pride,
that she showed promise of turning into
an arrestingly attractive young girl. Part
of her found pleasure for Mary's sake,
but the greater more primitive part of
her mother's heart took fright as she

realized the implications. Young men would soon find Mary and with every year that advanced Jackie must lose a little more of the girl's thoughts, affections, until at last she left him for the man she loved.

Ethel Bradbourne bottled these terrible fears for her son deep down inside her. She did not discuss them even with her husband, for she knew that Tom loved Mary almost as much as he loved Jackie . . . He had a deep pity for his helpless little son but no absorbing passion that might lead him to any action to avoid his being hurt. His was a more male affection and he had been able to take the tragedy of their child's accident and consequent abnormality more calmly than she had done, even while his disappointment must have been more acute. He had had such plans for sending his son to his own school, teaching him to play cricket, taking him mountain climbing, his own now neglected hobby.

Tom would advocate that Mary

should have her freedom. Had he been asked to discuss Mary's school report, he would most certainly have encouraged her to go to University, for he was a great believer in higher education for girls as well as boys. But by the time he learned of Mary's possibilities, the girl had already quite made up her mind that she wished to stay at home, and Tom accepted the decision as her choice.

'It *was* her choice,' the mother's voice whispered. 'I did not influence her. She loves Jackie. She said of her own accord she would never leave him!'

All the same, she knew that she had done wrong to let Mary grow up so completely selfless where Jackie was concerned. She should have guarded against the soft young heart giving too much many years ago. She should have seen that Mary had more friends . . . went out more . . . had more normal pursuits than merely seeing that Jackie was contented and happy. She had not exactly taken advantage of the girl's generous, loving disposition, but she had done nothing to guard against the future consequences. Her conscience smote her even while her heart argued that Jackie should never lack anything she could directly, or indirectly, give him.

'Well!' she told herself desperately. 'Mary has been to dances, parties, since she left school.' Tom had seen to that. He had made sure Mary was invited by the sons of his business friends to their homes. But even while Mary had enjoyed herself, she had always come home early, and lying awake in the darkness, her Aunt had gloried in the fact that Mary would go straight to Jackie's room, to smooth his pillow, to make sure he was sleeping comfortably and needed nothing.

After these parties, she would question her carefully about the other young people there. Mary would mention their names casually, simply, perhaps describing some boy she had danced with more often than with others, but so openly and without a flutter of an eyelash that her Aunt knew so far her heart had remained untouched and felt herself reprieved until the next time.

It never entered her mind to wonder about Mary's reactions to the new young doctor who had gone into partnership recently with their old Dr. Law. She had been so concerned about Jackie's health that she had given no thought to Mary. The boy had run a very high temperature for some days and was fretful and difficult and it had taken her and Mary's combined efforts to nurse and distract him. Dr. Law had himself succumbed to the epidemic and then young Dr. Deal had called in his place. By this time, she had herself caught a mild dose of the 'flu and retired to her bed. She did not feel well enough to appreciate that she was allowing into her house a very real potential danger to her child . . . for Paul Deal was not only young, but in a strong, masculine way exceedingly attractive. Moreover, he was unmarried.

But Mary, overworked as she was with two invalids in the house, had nevertheless found her heart beating curiously fast when the young doctor's startlingly blue, merry eyes looked across Jackie's bed into hers. She found herself thinking about him during the day, counting the hours till his next visit. A little surprised and amused, she discovered that she had taken greater pains than usual to brush her fair hair into a shining mass around her shoulders, to put on a freshly pressed skirt and her best 'twinset' with the several rows of bright pearls that had been her Uncle's last Christmas present to her.

Their conversation had been limited chiefly to sick-room instructions, for the young doctor had been desperately busy, with his elderly partner away and the epidemic at its worst. Nonetheless there had been something in his eyes, something which Mary could not but recognize as admiration and interest, and she was as happy about it as she was worried about Jackie and her Aunt. Her mind worried but her heart sang.

Today, when he had taken Jackie's temperature, pronounced him nearly better, and walked downstairs to the hall with Mary, he turned suddenly and said:

'You must be tired with so much to do. Yet you don't look it. You look . . . ' the blue eyes smiled a little mischievously, ' . . . wonderful!'

A swift blush spread over Mary's cheeks and her eyes went down to her hands, clasped together in front of her like a little girl's.

'You look about sixteen!'

She smiled then and said with a laugh:

'That is not a compliment. I was exceedingly plain at sixteen . . . thin, scraggy and typically school-girlish.'

Then she blushed again, realizing that he might suppose she imagined herself any different now.

The silence was broken when he said abruptly:

'Are you always tied to . . . to this house? I've never seen you about anywhere . . . at parties and dances, I mean.'

'Oh, I do go out sometimes!' Mary assured him. 'But I don't greatly enjoy social life . . . I'm rather shy, I suppose . . . or else just a home girl. I love looking after Jackie . . . even though he can be difficult sometimes.'

'But you're not his sister, are you? Dr. Law told me you were more or less adopted when you were a little girl.'

'Yes . . . my Aunt was my father's sister. When my parents died, they took me into their home and brought me up as their daughter. I've been very lucky, haven't I?'

He looked into those wide-open, candid brown eyes and felt his heart miss a beat. Was it possible for any young girl nowadays of nineteen, twenty, to be so completely selfless? Dr. Law had told him something of her life here with her Aunt and Uncle and the pathetic child she cared for so devotedly. He knew of the boy's dependence on her and had found himself blaming the Aunt for allowing this state of affairs to come about. Pity could be a terribly strong and powerful emotion, but love combined with it could be a cord that might tie this young girl always to a life for which she had not been destined. For surely so beautiful, so warm and compassionate a girl as stood before him now, was made to be a wife, a mother, a lover? Nature had made her as she was and some queer trick of Fate had placed her in a position where, if she stayed much longer, she could never hope to escape.

Yet it seemed to him that she had no wish to escape. All she did for Jackie she did willingly and without grudging the time spent. He had seen for himself how selfless was her devotion to the child. What would happen when she fell in love? For surely she had never been in love yet! Her innocence and her eyes told him she was unawakened to this most powerful of all emotions.

He shook his head and stooped to pick up his coat. Why should he worry about her? Why spend so much of these last few days since he had met her thinking about her? As he drove on his rounds he had caught himself wondering about her instead of his next patient's condition! Could he possibly be falling a little in love with her himself?

But no! There had been no time in his life for love. The six long years taken to complete his training as a doctor had left him with his degrees and a devotion and sense of dedication to the work he had chosen for himself, but little else. He had had one or two mild affairs . . . as had most of the students. He had imagined himself in love . . . but soon discovered that he was not. He told himself that it would be many years before he married . . . before he ceased to be too busy to be married. Now, at twenty-nine, he was not so sure of himself. He *had* been lonely. It was not enough, after all, to work all day and sometimes part of the night, with no one to be really interested in him or in his career; to have no interest, other than a medical one, in the other human beings around him. Dedicated as he had been to his work and to studying for further degrees, he had left himself no time for relaxation and enjoyment of the simpler things of life. In his way, he had been as tied as this girl must have been.

He turned at the front door and said suddenly:

'When this epidemic ends and Dr. Law is able to take on his own patients again, and your two invalids are up and about, will you come out with me one evening?'

'Why . . . I . . . I'd love to!' Mary said, the colour again rising into her cheeks.

'I don't know what you prefer to do . . . a concert? Opera? Theatre?'

'I'd love the theatre!' Mary said simply. 'I've only been twice . . . somehow there has never been time.'

'Yes, I know! But let's make time, shall we? I'll ring you up when things are easier.'

All day, Mary felt a glow in her heart . . . and a tiny nagging worry in case he had not really meant it . . . in case he would, after all, remain too busy . . . in case he forgot to ring.

2

In the week that followed, Mary knew herself to be in love. All through the long days, she found herself listening for the ring on the telephone . . . the ring that never came. Her bright expectancy changed to a dull lethargy and she went about her work without her usual smiling cheerfulness. Her Aunt noticed it and asked anxiously if she thought she was in for the 'flu. But Mary knew deep down inside her that she was just desperately disappointed. She had not realized until she was certain he would not ring how greatly she had counted upon his doing so, how much she wanted to see him again.

She made great efforts not to show her depression when she was with Jackie. He was so oddly sensitive to her moods and for no accountable reason would suddenly stroke her hand at a moment when she was sad or down-cast.

Paul Deal had not come to the house again in his medical capacity as Dr. Law had made a swift recovery and it was he who called to see the two convalescents. Mary found herself bringing Paul into the conversation.

'Jackie and I both liked your partner!' she said, knowing herself for a coward for including Jackie's name, although the boy *had* liked him and been far more responsive to him than he was to the doctor who had attended him most of his life. 'I hope he hasn't caught the 'flu?'

'No, indeed, he's in fine health!' Dr. Law said cheerfully as he removed the thermometer from Jackie's mouth and pronounced him fit enough to get up for an hour that afternoon. 'Nice young chap. I think I was lucky to get him, although I thought he was a bit young when he first applied for the partner-ship. But he has a good head on his shoulders and he's a hard worker all right! Nice-mannered, too.'

Mary had no doubt that he was good at his job; she had herself noticed the sureness of his hands and his quick summing up of the invalids. She had particularly liked his way with Jackie, gentle but firm . . . and he had treated him like any normal child. Dr. Law always behaved with him as if he could not understand anything at all, and since she had been a little girl, Mary had always resented this way some people had of treating Jackie . . .

She tried hard not to think about Paul Deal . . . not to say over again to herself the few brief personal words he had addressed to her. Could he have meant nothing by them after all? ' . . . you look wonderful! . . . but let's make time, shall we? I'll ring you up when things are easier!' She knew they must be 'easier' since Dr. Law was up and about again, but still he had not rung.

Then, on the eighth day, her Aunt called her to the telephone.

'It's young Dr. Deal; he wants to speak to *you*.'

Her eyes were on Mary's face as she delivered this curt comment and missed nothing of the quick flood of colour that raced into those pale cheeks. Her heart sank deep down with a sickening jolt. What could have gone on between those two while she had been lying ill in bed?

She handed the receiver into Mary's trembling hands and made pretence of leaving the room. But it was only a pretence for she knew that come what may, she MUST hear what the girl said . . . must know exactly what it was she had to fear. She recalled in a swift unhappy flash how good-looking the young doctor had been . . . tried to remember how many times he had called . . . how long he had stayed each time. Then her thoughts stopped as she overheard what she could of Mary's conversation.

'I'm sorry I've left it so long before telephoning. I've been trying to get seats for the new Terence Rattigan and I only heard this morning that I could have two cancellations. I thought you might particularly enjoy the play. It's very popular.'

'Of course! I'd love to go . . . I quite understand!' Mary said all in one breath. She was too happy . . . too immensely relieved to be able to conceal her state of mind.

'The seats are for Thursday . . . day after tomorrow . . . ' he went on. 'Shall we have supper afterwards? Then I can finish off my afternoon rounds and pick you up about five o'clock. Would that be all right?'

'It would be marvellous!' Mary said. 'Thank you very much — ' She broke off suddenly as she took in the full sense of his words . . . Thursday . . . the one day she couldn't manage . . . the one day when he had been able to get seats and she couldn't go.

'Anything wrong?'

'Oh, I'm afraid there is!' Mary cried, her disappointment acute and quite audible to the man at the other end of the wire. 'My Aunt and Uncle play bridge every Thursday evening and I stay in to mind Jackie ... I'm desperately sorry ... and after all your trouble, too.'

There was a moment of silence and then his voice came back to her:

'Isn't there someone else who could baby-sit that evening?'

Hope re-lit her face as she considered this straw.

'Well, once, last year, our daily came and sat in ... my Aunt and Uncle and I all went to a New Year Party ... but I don't know if Aunt Ethel would like it very much ... she always worries so ...'

'Then suppose I ask her? Can you call her to the telephone?'

'Yes, yes I will,' Mary cried ecstatically ... for she knew suddenly that she would have been afraid to ask her Aunt ... not because she would have been cross or angry but because she would have referred the question back to

Mary . . . 'Well, what do you think, dear? If *you* won't be worried and think Jackie will want you . . . then go and enjoy yourself!' She never would have gone . . . it would have left Jackie on her mind all evening.

She put down the phone and nearly knocked her Aunt over as she rushed through the open door into the hall.

'Dr. Deal wants to speak to you, Aunt Ethel!'

The older woman said:

'Oh! What does he want?'

With new-found tact, Mary remained silent and stood quietly waiting while her Aunt walked to the phone.

'Yes? . . . Oh . . . I see! Well, we never like to leave him with strangers, you know . . . yes, I admit he knows Mrs. King but . . . yes, but . . . oh, very well . . . ' and as if to rectify the ungraciousness of her tone of voice, she added: 'And thank you for asking Mary.'

She handed the telephone back to Mary with a brief: 'He wants to speak to you again!' and walked stiffly out of the room, knowing herself momentarily beaten. She began to dislike Paul Deal. She sensed the strong will that had adequately met and challenged her own . . . and won the first round. Without showing herself a complete despot, she could not have refused to let Mary go. Mrs. King *was* perfectly reliable . . . and Jackie was perfectly all right with her the few times they had had her in. It wasn't that she did not trust Mrs. King in this instance . . . it was that she did not trust Mary . . . or Paul Deal.

'Well, that's all fixed,' Paul was telling Mary calmly. 'I was sure your Aunt wouldn't refuse to let you go, particularly as you go out so seldom and to the theatre!'

'Thank you . . . thank you very much!' Mary said. 'I'll be looking forward to it so much.'

'So shall I! I shall hold thumbs furiously in case anything happens to hold me up. Just add to your prayers tonight, Mary, that nobody decides to have a baby on Thursday afternoon!'

She laughed with him, her eyes sparkling brightly. How nice his voice was . . . and he had called her 'Mary'! Could she call him Paul? With sudden daring she said:

'Good-bye, then, Paul. See you Thursday!'

He was grinning as he replaced the receiver. He had risked the 'Mary' and she had replied by shyly and charmingly calling him Paul . . . and his name had never sounded nicer! He felt wonderful . . . and knew that Mary was responsible. He had been to enough theatres in his day not to feel on top of the world because of that! It was Mary . . . quaint, shy, adorable Mary he wanted to see . . . not the actors on the stage. And he was pleased, too, with the firm way he had fixed that Aunt of hers.

His face hardened a little as he remembered Mrs. Bradbourne. He could see quite clearly that her one absorbing passion in life was the boy . . . poor little devil. And Mary was to be denied all her rightful heritage because the boy needed her. But not if he, Paul Deal, could prevent it. He had known of too many cases like this one where young and pretty girls on the threshold of life were forced to devote themselves to invalids and watch life pass them by, turning them into embittered old spinsters. Little Jackie was not Mary's child or her responsibility, and Mrs. Bradbourne should not permit her niece, her own flesh and blood, to sacrifice herself in this way. It was clear to see that she took advantage of Mary's love for the child, of her generosity and unselfishness. Had it not been for his own determination, Mary would have given up her Thursday outing without thought . . . but with considerable disappointment, he added to himself happily. Her tone of voice had not escaped him and he knew himself immensely happy at the thought that she really *wanted* to come. Could he dare hope that it was him she wished to see . . . rather than the play?

He knew now that he was at least a little in love. It seemed years since he had felt this way about any girl . . . and never quite this way . . . with never quite the warmth and protectiveness and sweetness that made up his feelings for Mary.

'She'd make a wonderful doctor's wife!' he told himself, and then laughed at himself for taking the last jump first. There were a great many hurdles . . . and difficult ones, he would have to cross first if this were to be his final intention. Mary's own feelings, for instance. She might not care for him at all . . . that way; and her Aunt . . . the child . . .

He could see many of the difficulties ahead that might bar his road to happiness if he pinned his hopes and thoughts on Mary. But right now he wasn't going to consider them . . . enough that he would be seeing her soon; not as her doctor but as her friend. And what a wonderful evening that would be!

Aunt Ethel was dreading that evening as greatly as Paul and her niece were longing for it. Conflict tore at her so that by the Thursday morning, the headache she had wondered if she dared fabricate became a real thing and she could retire to her bed without actually having to tell a lie. She kept her eyes closed when Mary came in with a hot water bottle and aspirins, for she was sufficiently human not to be able to look into the girl's anxious eyes and see there her fear and disappointment.

'Do you think you have the 'flu back, Aunt Ethel? Should I ask Dr. Law to come?'

'Oh, I don't think it's bad enough for that!' her Aunt said. 'I suppose it's a kind of relapse . . . I've been doing too much. But don't worry about me, Mary dear. You go off and iron your frock, or whatever it is you must do for your party tonight!'

'Oh, Aunt, darling, you know I'm wearing the wool jersey so it doesn't need ironing — ' She broke off suddenly as it occurred to her that she might at this last moment not be able to go.

'Aunt Ethel?' Her voice was taut and trembled a little. 'Would you feel happier if I stayed home?'

'Well, I'll admit I have been worrying a little about Jackie with Mrs. King . . . because he hasn't been well and is a bit fretful, isn't he? But I can manage . . . I can get up and go to him if he needs anything. You go and enjoy yourself, my dear!'

'But I don't think you ought to get out of a warm bed!' Mary heard her own voice saying automatically. 'Maybe I'd better stay . . . Jackie *has* been a bit off-colour today.'

'Oh, no, I can't have you giving up your fun just because I have a little chill.'

Hope and doubt tore alternately at Mary's heart. She couldn't NOT go . . . not now. For the last forty-eight hours she had thought of nothing else. It would be terrible . . . *terrible* to have to stay home now. Her Aunt couldn't be very ill or she would have allowed Dr. Law to come.

'Let me telephone Dr. Law!' she suggested again. 'I'm sure he wouldn't mind coming . . . just in case . . . '

'No!' her Aunt said firmly. 'I'm not ill. I can manage, Mary, so stop fussing. Go and have a good time.'

I ought not to go . . . I ought not to go, a voice kept repeating in Mary's ear, and yet she wanted to go so much . . . so very much. At lunch-time her Uncle came home and although she seldom discussed her feelings with him, she was so distraught with her mixed-up emotions, that she felt she had to talk it over with someone.

'I know I ought not to go, Uncle Tom, but you see, he went to such a lot of trouble to get tickets, seats, I mean, and it was only because of two cancellations that he managed it. I don't like to let him down . . . and . . . and I do rather want to go.'

Her Uncle looked at her in surprise.

It wasn't often that his quiet, collected little niece spoke with such emotion.

'But of course you'll go!' he said gruffly. 'I can see if your Aunt or Jackie need anything. I'm not helpless!'

Mary smiled.

'It isn't that, Uncle Tom . . . but you're playing bridge tonight. Aunt Ethel says they'll expect you even if she doesn't go.'

'Nonsense, my dear. What good is an odd man? They'd have to cut in and no one likes doing that. Anyway, I'd far rather stay at home . . . want to catch up on some letters. You toddle along and enjoy yourself, Mary. You deserve to have a gay time . . . spend too much of your time doing things for other people . . . enjoy yourself.'

Impulsively, Mary jumped up from her chair and went round the table to hug her Uncle. He had relieved her of making the decision and she really need not worry if he were going to stay home to look after her Aunt and Jackie.

'Who's the young man?' her Uncle

asked affectionately.

'Dr. Paul Deal!' Mary said shyly. 'He's awfully nice, Uncle.'

'Not a doddering old fuss-pot like Dr. Law, I hope?'

Mary laughed.

'Oh, no, Uncle! He's quite young . . . about thirty, I suppose . . . and . . . and very nice-looking. I met him when Dr. Law was ill and he came two or three times to see Jackie. Jackie liked him, too. Uncle, will it matter if I'm rather late home? We're having supper after the theatre as there won't be time before. I don't want you or Aunt to worry about me.'

'Be as late as you like, my dear . . . have a good time while you can. Got a key?'

'Yes, I have, Uncle!'

'Then let yourself in. We won't wait up. Trust you, you know, Mary. You're a good girl . . . know you wouldn't get up to any mischief. Got a pretty dress to wear?'

'Yes, Uncle Tom . . . the one you gave

me last Christmas . . . it's my favourite dress and I feel good in it.'

'Well, buy yourself something else with this . . . stockings or bag or whatever you want!' Her Uncle gave her a five pound note. 'And Mary?'

'Yes, Uncle?'

'If you find you like the chap, ask him back to dinner here one evening next week . . . like to meet him if you think so much of him — '

'But I never said — '

'No, but you look!' her Uncle teased her as he had been used to do when she was a little girl.

She flung her arms round him and kissed him on his cheek.

'I'm so happy . . . and so lucky to have you!' she sighed.

'And we're lucky to have you, my dear!' her Uncle said thoughtfully. 'Don't forget that. You've been a good girl . . . always, and anything we've ever done for you, you've more than repaid with what you have done for us. If you'd been our own daughter, you couldn't have done more. Now, what about the dessert? Aren't we having any today?'

After lunch, Mary took Jackie in his large push-chair for a walk in the gardens. Although it was November, the sun shone and there were plenty of children about. Mary and Jackie knew most of them for she brought him here nearly every day and the smaller children, having had their questions about 'the big boy in the pram' satisfactorily explained by their Nannies or parents, accepted him as being on their own level, and always came up to talk to him or catch the ball he would throw out of his pram with huge delight.

They fed the ducks on the ornamental pond and made their way home. As Mary unlocked the front door, she found herself hesitating to go in. Suppose there had been a telephone message for her to say Paul couldn't come? Only last week she had been in torment because the phone did not ring for her. Now she feared the opposite.

'Oh, don't let there be a baby now!' she prayed silently.

But there was no message on the hall pad and having given Jackie his tea and left him playing with his dinky cars with Mrs. King, she went in to see her Aunt.

'Are you feeling better?' she asked tentatively, trying to subdue her own bubbling happiness in this darkened room.

'My head still aches . . . but I'll be better tomorrow. Is Jackie all right?'

'Yes, he's playing with Mrs. King in the kitchen. She is staying on to put him to bed. Aunt Ethel . . . I . . . I want to thank you so much for letting me go . . . and for everything. You and Uncle Tom are always so good to me.'

'Well, for goodness' sake, child!' her Aunt said crossly. 'You sound as if you were going away for ever instead of to town for one evening!'

'I didn't mean it like that . . . ' Mary began and then stopped abruptly. Her Aunt was not feeling well and no doubt this accounted for her tone of voice. She had never before heard her so irritable . . . or so unloving. She must not be hurt by it.

'Is there anything I can get you?' she asked quietly.

'No, thank you. And, Mary, your Uncle said you might be late home . . . well, don't forget that it's Mrs. King's day off tomorrow and if I'm not well enough, you'll have to be up early to do the marketing.'

'I won't be very late. We're driving in Paul . . . Dr. Deal's car, so we shan't have to depend on the trains.'

She did not kiss her Aunt good-bye but left the room quietly, a faint unhappiness clouding her radiance of a moment before. But it did not last very long. As she bathed and slowly dressed herself with minute care and attention . . . and studied her reflection in the glass, the radiance returned and touched her eyes with stars so that she saw herself for the first time as beautiful . . . and gloried in it.

Then the front-door bell rang and a moment later she heard Paul's voice asking Mrs. King if Miss Mary was ready.

She slipped her smooth white arms into the softness of her fur coat, darted a last look in the mirror and curbing her haste she forced herself to walk slowly down the stairs.

3

'Tell me about yourself, Mary!' Paul asked her as they drove slowly and carefully through the suburbs towards the West End of London.

'Oh, no! I'd rather we talked about you . . . you must have had such an interesting life!' Mary said shyly. Ever since she had caught his gaze on her as she came down the stairs and read in his expression something . . . well, special . . . a kind of intimacy that was different from the casual complimentary glances of the other boys or young men she had encountered, she had felt her heart thudding so fiercely in her breast that she had wondered if Paul could hear it. Then a moment later as he put his arm lightly through hers and bade Mrs. King good night, she began to doubt that there *had* been anything special in that look.

Uncertain of herself and of him or even of what she wanted of him, she had been unable to make light conversation during the first five minutes of the drive and had left it to Paul to talk about the baby which had fortunately arrived that morning! Now he had asked her about herself, but she didn't wish to talk of her life which she considered to be eventless and commonplace. She wanted to hear about him.

'Please!' she said. 'I don't know anything at all about you except that you are Dr. Law's new partner and that he thinks very highly of you!'

'Well, thanks to Dr. Law for his kind remarks. I'm glad he gave me a good press. All the same, there isn't much to tell about myself.'

'There must be something!' Mary replied, smiling. 'Pretend you have just climbed Everest and I'm a reporter asking you for something about you to put in my paper.'

He turned his head for an instant to

glance down at the face beside him. What a strange and attractive mixture this girl was . . . half child still, half woman. In her fur coat with that soft woolly dress he had glimpsed beneath it, draped charmingly over her shoulders and across her firm young bosom, she looked wholly woman, and very beautiful to him. He had watched her descend the stairs with a great longing to go forward and hold out his arms to her . . . to draw her down against him and to kiss those delicately curved lips, smiling shyly at him as she murmured some greeting.

Dr. Law told him she was twenty. So he knew that in her body she was mature . . . yet her life had been so secluded, it seemed, and she herself so inexperienced that her mind and emotions were still those of a young girl. Unawakened! And to whom would go the glory of seeing those eyes awakening to love? Dare he hope . . . ?

He pulled himself up sharply and said:

'Well, I was born twenty-nine years ago in Devonshire. I am one of a family of six, three boys and three girls. My father was and still is a doctor and I always intended to follow in his footsteps, although my family were not sure that they would be able to afford my training. But I worked like a demon at school and won a scholarship and got my heart's desire ... my medical training in Edinburgh. That took six long years. After I'd qualified I went to a hospital in London for a year and then having made up my mind I wanted to be a G.P. and not a surgeon or a specialist, I got an assistant's job down in Devon near my home. I stayed there four years and eventually heard Dr. Law wanted a junior partner, so I applied and got the job. I arrived three months ago. That's all there is to say about me.'

'But there is more!' Mary suggested. 'Tell me about your family. It must be fun having so many brothers and sisters.'

'Well, we've always been a very united family. My mother saw to that, I think. She's a wonderful woman . . . managed to be the perfect wife for father and mother and friend to all of us as well.'

'How did she find the time?'

'I don't know. She was always busy, of course, but as we grew older, we all helped a bit . . . took turns to wash up and made our own beds and that kind of thing. Mother said it would do us boys the world of good . . . preparing to be good husbands! My sister Jean is secretary to our local M.P. My younger brother, Neal, is following in my footsteps and in the middle of his training. The next girl is at her last term at school and wants to be a nurse and the two youngest are still at school alternating between wanting to be train drivers, Range Riders and Florence Nightingale!'

'I suppose you don't see much of them?' Mary asked.

'Twice a year . . . when I take leave.

Perhaps . . . I suppose it wouldn't be possible for you to come down with me at Christmas? Or if you prefer to spend Christmas with your relations, then for the New Year? I'm getting ten days from twenty-fourth to the third. We always give a dance at New Year and I think you'd enjoy it.'

'It sounds perfect!' Mary said, glowing. 'But I'm still more or less a stranger to you and a complete stranger to your family. Maybe they wouldn't want me staying, specially at such a time as Christmas.'

'They'd love it. And within ten minutes I guarantee you'll not feel or be a stranger to them . . . not with my young brothers and sisters around.'

Mary dreamed a moment longer . . . then reality came to the fore and she said:

'I would have loved it . . . I know I would. But, of course, I couldn't get away for two or three days.'

'But why ever not?' he asked incredulously.

48

'Well, Jackie depends on me for nearly everything. I don't mean to feed him, of course, because he manages very well now. But to entertain him . . . take him out for walks . . . that kind of thing.'

'But, Mary . . . ' her name slipped out quite easily this time, 'he must learn some time that you will not always be at his beck and call. Two or three days won't hurt him and he has his mother.'

'But . . . I know it seems queer to think of it . . . he really much prefers to be with me. I think Aunt Ethel is too . . . too intense with him. She worries so about him and that frightens him.'

'Perhaps because he has never learned to trust her as he trusts you. He must learn sometime!' Paul reiterated.

'But I shan't ever leave him!' Mary cried spontaneously. 'I *couldn't*. He'd be miserable . . . I couldn't!'

'Don't you ever intend to get married?'

The question was one Mary had never allowed herself to stop and

49

consider. Once or twice she had thought about it . . . and pushed the thought away quickly . . . just as she had rejected the thought that had once concerned her with University. She was young yet . . . there were many years before she would want to marry . . . time enough then to think about it.

But now Paul had voiced the thought . . . and voiced the half-dreams that had troubled her mind these last weeks. Suppose she *did* want to marry one day? What would happen to Jackie?

She had spoken the last thought aloud and he answered her quickly.

'He will be perfectly all right, Mary. He has the mind of a child of four or five. Children of that age are adaptable . . . and he will soon learn to depend on his mother for the things you give him now. You must not throw your life away on a useless sacrifice . . . useless because it is quite unnecessary.'

'Perhaps you're right!' Mary agreed. 'But I won't think about it now . . . I want to enjoy myself this evening

. . . forget everything else but . . . '
quickly she changed the 'you' she had
been going to say to . . . 'about the play
and supper afterwards.'

The man beside her knew now that
one day he would ask this girl to be his
wife . . . knew it as certainly as he knew
the road into London. Thinking about
it afterwards, he could not fathom why
he had suddenly had this knowledge at
this particular moment, but from then
onwards, he had no doubts as to his
future. He did not think about love
. . . or being in love . . . only that it was
not necessary to pursue the subject of
Jackie at this stage. There would be
time enough later. Nothing else would
matter except that Mary should have
the most perfect evening of her life
. . . and learn to care for him a little.

He found pleasing her delightfully
easy. She went out so seldom, that she
was like a child on a school treat
. . . glowing, happy, enchanted. And as
he watched her face instead of the play
enacted on the stage, he found himself

every moment a little more entranced by her, a little more amazed that in this century any girl of twenty could be so completely unsophisticated and unspoiled. She had the charm of innocence and the graceful mature dignity of a woman. All her gestures were coordinated and smooth-flowing . . . there was nothing gawky or awkward about her . . . and yet her words were young and full of enthusiasm and spontaneity.

Mary had indeed lost herself in the play. She even momentarily forgot the man beside her except in the interval when she went with him to the foyer for a cup of coffee and thought how nicely mannered he was, how charming and considerate.

But she became fully aware of him again when they climbed once more into his car and he leant across her to tuck a light rug round her knees. As he did so, his hand touched hers accidentally, then suddenly found and held it.

'Cold!' he almost whispered. 'Put my

gloves on, Mary!'

His words were like a caress and the touch of his hands as he slid his own fur-lined gloves over her fingers sent a strange burning fire right through her body. She was trembling and hoped he wouldn't notice. She could not trust her voice and so remained silent.

'I think we'll go to Quaglino's,' Paul said, as he pushed the self-starter to cover his own surprising emotion. 'We can dance there if you care to.'

'I love dancing!' Mary murmured. 'But I'm afraid I'm not very good . . . I don't get much practice, you see.'

'I love it, too. Don't worry about it, Mary. We'll get along fine, I know it.'

Because she was so sure of it too, she felt too deeply happy and content for words. She sat silently beside him, every now and again stealing a glance at the firm profile of the man beside her. Once he turned his head and, catching her eye, smiled his quick boyish grin. She felt her heart jolt and was glad that the bright London lights could not fully reveal the colour that had such a tell-tale way of rushing into her cheeks.

Mary was a little uncertain of herself when they first went through the door into the smart restaurant where he had chosen to dine. But her companion was so thoughtful of her that she had no chance to do the wrong thing. He indicated where she should go to leave her coat and told her exactly where he would be waiting when she came back.

She lingered a little as she touched up her make-up, just in case she might arrive before him, but he was waiting as he had promised, and a few moments later they were seated at a small table a little way from the dance floor.

'This is fun!' Mary sighed, closing her eyes and drawing a deep breath . . . afraid that she might after all wake up and discover she had been dreaming.

Paul ordered dinner for them both . . . again relieving her of any difficulty she might have had with the French menu. Then, while they waited for it to arrive, Paul suggested they should dance.

Nervously, Mary preceded him onto the floor, wishing she had had more practice and hoping desperately that she would not force him to stumble over her toes. But within a few seconds she knew she need not worry. Paul was the most perfect dancer in the world and no one with any sense of rhythm could help follow him. A moment more and she could relax and cease to worry about her steps, and it was then he drew her suddenly close against him and bent his head so that his cheek touched hers.

'Mary, you're so pretty!' he whispered. 'I've been longing to do this all evening!'

Mary had not consciously considered it before, but she knew now that this was where she had always wanted to be . . . in his arms. Her whole life up to this moment had been no more than a long period of waiting for this moment . . . for these unbearably beautiful emotions that swept through her in thrilling waves. She was utterly without coquetry and made no attempt to withdraw her cheek from his, but leant against him more closely as if it were the most natural thing in the world to be doing. She wanted to be near him and that was enough since he wanted it, too.

Her softness, her lightness, the sweetness of her hair and perfume, tore into Paul's heart. His arm tightened about her and he knew by the brief touch of her long dark lashes that her eyes were closed. The longing utterly to possess her became suddenly unbearable for him and he loosened his hold of her and said with difficulty:

'You're a lovely dancer, Mary. You had no need to be afraid!'

She tore herself out of the deep whirlwind of emotions that had had her completely entranced and tried to answer him in the same light tone he had used to her. But she was not experienced enough yet to control her emotions so quickly and her hand trembled in his own. Instantly his fingers tightened about hers and he said again: 'Mary, Mary . . . how pretty you are!'

No one had ever behaved in just this way with her before. In the jumble of her thoughts, Mary tried to remember other young men she had met. There had been Derek . . . he had told her she was pretty . . . that he was more than half in love with her . . . but somehow it had just sounded meaningless . . . and she had laughed and teased him a little and told him it was just the moonlight. He had kissed her afterwards but it had meant nothing and she had forgotten all about it until this moment. If Paul were to kiss her . . . she could never, never forget. She would remember it all her life . . . just as she would remember the soft caressing tones of his voice as he said: 'Mary, Mary, you're so pretty!'

But Paul's thoughts had gone a long way beyond kisses. He knew that he loved the girl in his arms . . . loved her with all his senses, mental and physical. Her nearness was a sweet yet unbearable temptation to him. He knew that he had been swept completely off his feet and must try to find a firm footing if he was to behave at all reasonably for the rest of the evening.

As he took her back to their table, he tried to keep the conversation light and amusing and soon she was laughing at him from those astonishing dark eyes of hers.

'How did you come by that unusual combination of dark eyes and fair hair?' he asked her. 'It's . . . bewitching, Mary.'

She smiled at him, suddenly shy as she seemed always to be when he paid her a compliment.

'My mother was Norwegian and I have her fair hair. My eyes are my father's. My parents were visiting friends of Mother's in Norway when they were killed in a sailing accident. I was only a very little girl at the time so I don't remember anything about it

. . . and I only know what Aunt Ethel has told me of my parents. To me she and Uncle Tom have been Mother and Father, although I don't call them that.'

'What a shame your real parents could not have lived to see you as you are tonight. They would have been so proud!'

'You say such nice things!' Mary whispered. 'I'll be going home tonight with a very swollen head. I . . . I think your parents must be very proud of you, too!'

Paul laughed.

'Well, I expect they are, being ordinary parents who think their offspring the most perfect in the world. All the same, I'm one of six, don't forget, so I only come in for a sixth of their adulations!'

They danced again, but Paul did not hold her close against him and Mary felt a little of her intense pleasure giving way to a tiny fear. Was he a little bored with her now? He must have so many interesting and clever women friends

. . . beautiful, too. Beautiful women would not hesitate to notice Paul . . . he was so exceptionally handsome . . . and it had not escaped her notice how several women at other tables had turned to stare a little at him. Mary was so completely without conceit that it did not occur to her that their partners were also looking their way . . . at her, and that their flattering remarks could refer to both . . . admiring their good looks and commenting on their 'rightness' together.

When Mary glanced at her wrist-watch and discovered it was midnight, she gave a little gasp of dismay.

'I'll have to go home right away, Paul. I'd no idea it was so late.'

'You're just like Cinderella!' Paul teased her.

'It's just that I promised Aunt Ethel —'

'Oh, hang Aunt Ethel!' Paul broke in involuntarily and then they both laughed.

'I really should go, all the same!' Mary said. 'It will take us half an hour to get back, won't it? And I have to be up early tomorrow to do the week-end shopping.'

Obediently, Paul beckoned the waiter. While Mary went to collect her coat, he paid the bill and stood waiting for her, thinking a little angrily about Mary's life. She seemed not to be aware of it, yet to him it was quite clear that her Aunt made use of her and treated her like a servant, arranging and controlling her life and keeping her tied to the sick child. Had Mary really no ambitions beyond nursing Jackie and doing the shopping for her Aunt? How could she accept such bondage without question? She had shown herself remarkably intelligent during their varied conversation tonight. She had a quick, receptive and well-informed brain . . . she could have gone far in any direction had she chosen. It seemed such a waste until he remembered it was her very innocence and guilelessness that had first attracted him to her. If she had been around in the world she would not, at twenty, be

61

as she was tonight. He recalled his own twenty-two-year-old sister, Jean . . . by comparison years older than Mary and with two not very serious love-affairs already behind her and a third young man in tow. Somehow he was aware that Mary had never been in love . . . that this evening he had opened her eyes and heart a little to the bitter-sweet joys of loving.

They were both quiet during the drive home . . . talking only occasionally about the road or the traffic. But it was a companionable silence and Mary was deeply and utterly happy. It had been a perfect evening . . . quite perfect and she would not change one second of it.

She told him so as the car turned into the corner of the road in which her Aunt's house stood, dark and strange-looking seen at this late hour.

Paul Deal dropped his hands from the driving wheel and turned to look at the girl sitting so motionless beside him. His heart jolted uncomfortably and he felt the tension mounting as he made no reply. Suitable words to tell her all that he was feeling, would not come to his lips. Slowly, inexorably, he lifted his arms, and drew the waiting girl swiftly against him. A moment later his lips were on hers and Mary knew for the second time the delirious magic that must always exist for her at his touch.

'I love him, I love him!' she thought as her heart thundered its beat and her arms went round his neck to draw him even closer to her. The gesture was spontaneous and made from the demands of her heart and body and she was herself shaken by the sudden gust of passion that tore through them both at this proximity. Paul's kisses covered her mouth, her eyes, her hands and then her lips again.

'Mary, Mary!' he whispered over and over again, until at last, with a little groan, he drew himself away from her and held only her two hands in his own. They stared into each other's eyes, surprised, moved beyond words, then very tenderly and slowly, Paul's blue eyes crinkled into a half smile and a little tremulously, Mary smiled back at him.

'It's all been quite perfect . . . ' she whispered again, hesitantly. '*All* of it!' And he knew that she meant these last minutes, too.

'Darling Mary! I'll ring you!' he promised. 'Tomorrow!'

Very gently, he kissed her good night . . . just a feather-weight touch of his lips on hers, for he dare not trust himself to kiss her more deeply a second time. Never had he felt such a galaxy of emotions before. The touch of Mary's lips, a glance from those dark eyes of hers, sent the blood whirling madly through him and a confusion of tenderness and desire warring within him.

'Of course, I'm in love!' he told himself without any great surprise and he drove slowly back to his digs. He had known it ever since he first met her.

Now he was quite sure. And he was a little afraid of what it might mean. He could no longer deny those questions about the future. It mattered now so much that he could not shelve the thoughts that crowded his mind. For even if Mary came to love him as he loved her, could any man come between her and her sense of love and duty to her cousin, or was it to that Aunt?

'Love between a man and a woman is the most powerful of all emotions,' he told himself reassuringly. 'If she loves me, she'll come to me.'

But he had not made sufficient allowance for another kind of love . . . perhaps even more powerful and enduring . . . that of a woman for her child.

In the darkness, Mrs. Bradbourne lay awake, hearing Mary climb the stairs and close her bedroom door. She heard Paul's car restart, just as she had heard it stop and suffered a lifetime of agony at the silence that ensued. She knew as surely as if she could see them that they were kissing each other good night . . . knew that she had everything to fear for the future.

'I'll never let her leave Jackie, *never*!' she vowed into the darkness, knowing that her thoughts were evil and wrong, but convincing herself paradoxically that because of Jackie they were right.

4

Mary spent the following morning shopping. She felt a little tired but her inner happiness kept her buoyant and light-hearted and she hardly noticed her tiredness. She hurried through her shopping list as fast as she could, suddenly afraid that Paul might telephone while she was out.

But when she returned home, her Aunt made no mention of a call and Mary was suddenly too shy to ask. There seemed to be a new relationship between herself and her Aunt . . . a queer kind of tension that Mary was unable to account for. Her Aunt had always been affectionate to her and had seemed to go out of her way to do little things to please Mary and make her happy. Mary could not put her finger on any one thing which proved a change of heart but she felt a new emotion in her Aunt's presence . . . a discomfort, a shyness and a faint stirring of anxiety.

'You're sure you're well enough to be up and about?' she asked with her usual solicitude.

'Do stop fussing, Mary!' her Aunt said crossly and Mary was hurt and a little dismayed by that same irritable tone of voice she had first heard last night. It was true her Aunt did not look well. She was an attractive woman of forty, petite in build and essentially dainty in her gestures and stature. Her hair had turned grey after Jackie's tragic accident but she had it cut short and blued and it was always perfectly dressed. She looked more like Mary's elder sister than her Aunt and people had often remarked upon it. But this morning she looked her age. There were dark shadows beneath her eyes and creases in her forehead and a tight-drawn line on either side of her mouth.

Mary was not to know that her Aunt was in an agony of mind. Sooner than she had expected, her first test had come. Paul Deal had telephoned to speak to Mary and left a message for her to ring back when she returned from her shopping. Her Aunt had decided not to deliver that message. It might not be in the least important what they would say to each other, but the very fact that the young doctor had telephoned so early indicated *his* state of mind, and she knew that love can beget love, even if Mary were immune as yet. There was a look about the young girl at the breakfast table that had disproved her immunity . . . indescribable but there . . . a kind of radiance and special beauty that comes to women in love.

Of course, her Aunt could not expect her failure to pass on Paul's message to go unnoticed. No doubt Paul would telephone again and tell Mary it was for the second time. But there was just a chance that he might not . . . that he could be led to suppose Mary was not interested in him. Pride might prevent him ringing a second time.

What she had not taken into account was that her action might only serve to increase Mary's desire to hear from Paul, his to hear from her. And at lunch-time, Paul phoned again.

'Mary?'

'Paul! How nice of you to ring so soon. I've been wanting to thank you for last evening ... I had such a wonderful time.'

'So did I! I rang you earlier but you were out. Did you not get my message to ring me back or were you too busy?'

Mary frowned a little.

'Your message? No, I didn't get it. Perhaps my Aunt forgot.' Uneasiness stirred within her, but her happiness at talking to Paul surmounted it.

'Never mind. Tell me when I can see you again.'

Remembering Uncle Tom's suggestion, Mary said breathlessly:

'My Uncle thought you might like to have dinner here with us one evening next week. Could you manage it?'

Paul had no real wish to spend the evening sharing her with her Aunt and Uncle, but he realized that he must make the necessary acquaintance with her relatives and it might as well be done sooner as later. At least he would see Mary and maybe he could find a moment to be alone with her.

'I'd love to,' he said.

'Would Tuesday be all right?' Mary asked him.

'I may be rather late . . . I have an evening surgery on Tuesday.'

'Wednesday, then? I don't think my Aunt or Uncle are doing anything either day, so you can choose.'

'Let's make it Wednesday then . . . and, Mary, did you ever see *Genevieve*? The film, I mean?'

'No, I didn't!' Mary said.

'Well, it's on at the local cinema the last three days of the week, I missed it before and I've heard it is most amusing. What about coming to see it on Saturday?'

Mary sighed contentedly as she replaced the receiver after Paul's 'good-bye'. She would see him Wednesday and Saturday. Life was perfect . . . and the most perfect thing of all was that he seemed to want to see her as much as she wanted to see him. Admittedly there were four days to be lived through before next Wednesday; but she could wait; even the waiting had its own enchantment when she could dream of the joys in store just as she could dream of the glory of last night.

'Mary, Jackie's calling you . . . couldn't you hear him?'

Her Aunt's voice brought her guiltily back to the present and with a little flush on her cheeks, Mary ran quickly up the stairs.

The boy was fractious at first. He had wanted Mary to come and amuse him and she had been out shopping.

'Why didn't you take me with you?' he asked querulously. 'I wanted to go, too!'

But gradually Mary's radiant happiness passed on to the child who, as always, was receptive to her moods and sensitive to the atmosphere around him; soon he was laughing gaily and they were planning their afternoon walk.

As she pushed the big pram round the gardens later that day, Mary found herself stopping to consider the future. What could it bring her? What did she want of life? For Paul Deal to fall in love with her! But if he did, what then? Did she want to marry him? True, she hardly knew him . . . they had only met a half-dozen times, yet already she felt she must always have known him. She no longer tried to deny to herself that she was in love with him. And if he returned that love and asked her to marry him? Would she want to be his wife?

Yes, yes, yes! Mary's heart told her. But what of Jackie? She *couldn't* leave him. She had promised her Aunt she would never do so and her own sense of dedication and loyalty and love for the child bound her to that promise. Jackie needed her . . . he was only really happy when she was with him. She could not walk out and desert him.

Yet she could not give up her whole life. Surely she was entitled to love . . . to marriage . . . to children of her own! They were every woman's right. It might seem enough now just to have Paul love her . . . but would it always be enough? She would want more . . . just as he would want more, and then, when she must deny him and herself, he would grow tired of her. He, too, had a right to love and marriage.

She tried to calm her thoughts by assuring herself that she was crossing bridges long before she came to them. There had been no mention of love between them and here she was thinking about marriage and babies! Paul probably meant nothing at all by his kisses. She knew enough of the world to know that kisses were in no way binding these days . . . that most men kissed the girls they took out if the girls let them. Yet somehow she had been made to feel there was something more than just a passing attraction ... she had felt a good deal more herself. And the warmth of his voice when he had spoken on the telephone ... so many little things led up to her belief in his interest in her.

'I won't think about the future!' she told herself firmly. 'I won't let anything spoil my happiness.'

But she did think a lot about Paul and the future and gradually the first brightness and glory of her dreams became clouded with the very worries she had determined not to face. What *would* happen to Jackie if she ever wanted to marry? Her Aunt would have to get some kind of Nanny or governess to help her care for him and he'd hate that ... or at least until he got used to someone else. Besides, her Aunt had always sworn she would never have another one. Since he could remember, Jackie had never had anyone but Mary to minister to his needs and he would be terribly upset; it might even set him back; make him ill. Yet if she were to marry someone like Paul whose practice was in the district, she could see Jackie every day . . . take him out for his walk herself . . . call in whenever he needed her . . .

She discovered that when she tried to think dispassionately about her future, she found all her plans centering around Paul Deal and knew herself for a fool. They had met so few times, knew so little of each other. It was madness to consider marriage when for all she knew he had only a mild interest in her!

But when at last Wednesday came and Paul arrived to dinner, she felt her confidence return. There was something in the expression of his eyes when he greeted her . . . something in the tone of his voice when he addressed her . . . something that must surely mean he had waited as anxiously as herself for this evening to come.

Her Aunt had shown no enthusiasm

for this family dinner party, but Mary had excused her Aunt's behaviour as being general depression following her 'flu. Her Uncle, however, had teased her gently about her 'young man' and was undoubtedly putting himself out to be pleasant. He kept Paul back at the table for a glass of his special brandy and Mary found herself alone in the sitting-room with her Aunt. For the first time in her life, Mary wished that her own Mother sat there with her . . . not her Aunt with whom she seemed so strangely and suddenly to have lost touch. Up until now she had always been able to confide in Aunt Ethel, voice her childish hopes and thoughts and been kindly dealt with. But there was an unresponsiveness, a hardness about the older woman that chilled Mary and left her feeling unhappy and alone. She longed so to confide in some other woman the unbearable fullness of her feelings. She had no girl-friend near enough in sympathy with her to whom she could talk about Paul to her heart's content.

Mrs. King, who had stayed to cook and serve the dinner, brought in the coffee tray and said good night. When she had gone, Mrs. Bradbourne turned to her niece and said:

'Your doctor is older than I expected, Mary. He must be quite ten years older than you.'

'Oh, no, Aunt Ethel, only nine!' Mary replied, and became instantly aware that her Aunt must realize she had already counted the difference in their ages.

'Well, that's almost as much!' Her tone of voice was nearly sarcastic. Mary again felt a little chill at her spine. 'I wonder he hasn't already married, but then of course he has probably been busy studying. I can't say I would envy his wife . . . any doctor's wife . . . never a moment to oneself . . . always at the beck and call of patients every hour of the day and night.'

'But Paul says his mother has been terribly happy all her life . . . his father is a doctor . . . and he has five brothers and sisters ——'

She broke off, hating herself for being on the defensive and wishing that Paul and her Uncle would return. Didn't Aunt Ethel like him? How could she not do so? He had been utterly charming to her all evening and there could have been nothing to which she might object. Could she be worrying in case she and Paul were falling in love?

The thought hit Mary with the force of a physical impact and momentarily she caught her breath. *Naturally* her Aunt would be worried, disturbed by such a thought . . . she would worry about Jackie.

With all that was generous and loving in her nature coming to the fore, Mary stood up and went to her Aunt, putting her arms about the rigid shoulders and gently touching her lips to the older woman's hair.

'Dear Aunt Ethel!' she murmured. 'Please don't ever worry about the future. I'll never walk out of Jackie's life whatever happens. He is as dear to me as he is to you. Don't worry about it, will you?'

The thin line of her Aunt's lips slackened a little as if Mary had managed at last to break down her defences as she had surprised on the truth of her thoughts. She seemed to Mary to be about to speak when they heard the men's voices and she went back to her own chair as they came into the room.

'I've been talking to your Uncle about the New Year!' Paul said as Mrs. Bradbourne poured out coffee. 'He thinks you should certainly have a few days to come and visit my family if you would like to. He's going to speak to your Aunt!'

Mary had not forgotten the suggestion that she should go to Devon and her heart beat furiously at the thought that Paul had not only meant it but already spoken to her Uncle about it.

'I would love it!' she said quietly, and then they moved apart as her Aunt came forward with the coffee.

Paul had mentioned the news to her because he was anxious . . . surprisingly anxious . . . to learn if he could count upon her to come. He knew quite surely that if she did not want to come, he would lose all his usual pleasure and excitement in going home. And he had not been sure if he would have another moment alone with her in which to speak of it. He could, of course, have spoken in front of Mrs. Bradbourne, but something in the older woman's attitude to him betrayed her inner hostility even while her manners were impeccable, and Paul had recognized a potential enemy. He was wise enough to realize the cause for she could surely have nothing else against him. Mary was twenty and quite old enough to be meeting young men and going out to dances and parties or staying with their families. It was true that he was older than she by nine years, but that was not such a bad thing between a man and a woman. Besides, his position as a doctor was assured and he had Dr. Law's 'protection' as being socially acceptable, even if his manner and his ability and profession were not surety enough. Without vanity, he could not accept that her antagonism was to himself personally . . . but to any prospective husband Mary might find for herself.

'But two can play her game!' he thought. 'I'll not let her hold Mary a prisoner all her life. And if Mary loves me, I'll win in the end.'

Uncle Tom seemed to be on Paul's side! With nice tact, he insisted that he and his wife wanted an early night, and at ten o'clock he announced that they were off to bed and would Mary turn off the lights when she came up.

'I'd better be getting along, too,' Paul said reluctantly, but Uncle Tom shook his head.

'I know you lads . . . ten o'clock was early to me at your age. Help yourself to another drink, young man, and keep Mary company. She won't want to be off to bed yet!'

Mrs. Bradbourne was powerless under the circumstances to do anything else but follow her husband out of the room. She turned her cheek to Mary's kiss and her good night to Paul was barely polite in its abruptness. But Uncle Tom shook his hand warmly and said:

'Come again when you have the time, my boy . . . enjoyed having you . . . come again!'

'I do like your Uncle!' Paul said as he settled himself down again in the armchair by the fire. 'He must be quite a young man for all he talks as if he were my father!'

'Well, he's a good deal older than Aunt Ethel . . . I think he's nearly fifty-five!' Mary said, and remembered suddenly that her Aunt had quibbled at nine years! There were fifteen between her and the man *she* had married!

The thought made her blush and Paul, watching her, smiled and said quickly:

'A penny for them, Mary!'

But she would not tell and only blushed deeper.

'Come and sit over here by the fire!' Paul said. 'You're much too far away over there . . . besides, it's cold under that window.' And as she moved towards him, he added: 'Here, lean against my knees and toast your toes!'

Obediently, she sat on the fireside rug and leant back against him, and instantly felt his hand on her head. Knowing he could not see her face, her eyes closed and she thought:

'Paul, Paul, I love you, I love you!'

As if aware of her heart's cry, Paul said softly:

'Do you know I'm in love with you, Mary? I didn't mean to speak of it so soon, but I can't help it. Each time I see you I am a little more certain about it. Does it surprise you? Turn your face, my darling, so that I can see your eyes!'

His words, the endearment, the tenderness of his voice, all brought a little involuntary cry from her lips. She turned towards him and laid her cheek against his hand.

'Paul ... I love you, too!' she whispered tremulously. 'At least, I think it must be love. I think of you all day and half the night. I've never been in love before!'

Not altogether surprised, but deeply and profoundly touched by the simplicity of her admission, Paul drew her upwards so that she lay across his knees, held tightly against his heart. She seemed suddenly to be very small and fragile and childlike as he held her there a moment before bending his head to kiss her upturned mouth. His tenderness and love for her were almost more than he could bear and she felt his emotion in that kiss.

'Paul, I'm so lucky ... that it should be you!' she voiced her thoughts when the kiss ended. 'You're so wonderful to me!'

'Darling, how could any man help being wonderful to you? Do you realize how sweet you are? How unique?

There's no one in the world quite like you, Mary. You're such a strange combination of child and woman . . . it's irresistible.'

She smiled softly . . . a woman's smile.

'Have you known so many women, that you can say that and be sure?' she teased him.

He kissed her again, three times, lightly and humorously.

'No, but I'm still sure. Maybe it is something to do with your Norwegian mother and English father. Mary, the family are going to love you . . . I know it. I'm so happy you'll come at the New Year!'

She snuggled closer against him, all child now as she said:

'Tell me some more about them, Paul. There's so much of your life I've missed.'

'I'll show you all the family photograph albums and that will bring you right up to date!' Paul laughed happily. Then his face grew more serious and he looked deep into those dark eyes of hers as he said: 'Mary, if you still feel the same way at the New Year, will you let me announce our engagement? Will you marry me?'

Even while her heart thrilled at his words, her first proposal and the only one she ever wanted to hear ... the same disquieting worry came back to destroy the perfection of her happiness. To be engaged ... to be married. The first meant the second *and what of Jackie?*

'You don't answer me, Mary? Aren't you sure you love me? Have I rushed you too much?'

'It isn't that!' Mary whispered. 'I know I love you, Paul ... I know I always will. And I want to be engaged to you ... to be married sometime. But it is unexpected ... I haven't thought very deeply about marriage. You see, I never supposed I would want to get married ... but then I've never been even close to being in love before ... and, Paul, there's Jackie. He needs me.'

'I know!' Paul answered her quietly. 'But I shall need you, too, Mary. I need you now. I never realized quite how lonely and pointless my life seemed till this last week. I want you for my wife, Mary. I want you in every way!'

Carried away by his feelings, he kissed her feverishly and with far more passion than he had hitherto allowed himself to show. Mary, awakening for the first time to the force of her own desires, responded shyly yet with her whole heart. Each touch of his hands was a strange half-painful magic that started fires she had never in her innocence dreamed of. Fearful and yet responsive, she gave him back kiss for kiss with all the ardour of her warm nature. The tension grew until Mary felt all thought cease and knew only the sweet longing of sensation.

It was fortunate that Paul, moved and trembling as he was by his love for her and hers for him, was yet fully in control of himself, and beyond anything he might desire for himself, he desired to protect and guard Mary, such was the profoundness, the quality of his love for her. When at last he released his hold of her and she stood shakily on her own feet once more, he glanced at her flushed cheeks and star-bright eyes and knew that the girl he had chosen was really his true love. The fires he had awakened in her were akin to his own, for all her sweet innocence.

'I do love you so much!' he told her. 'Don't let anything come between us, Mary!'

At that moment, Mary felt that nothing in the whole world mattered but Paul. Nothing *could* come between them! And yet later, she remembered Jackie . . . the poor little boy, her cousin, who through no fault of his own must be dependent all his life, and whose dependence and happiness lay more on her shoulders than on anyone else's. How then could she marry Paul?

5

Mrs. Bradbourne was ill again. An acute migraine had sent her back to bed and her sufferings were by no means imaginary. She allowed Mary to call Dr. Law, who could do very little for her except tell her to remain in a darkened room and take a mild sedative.

'You're not worrying about anything, Ethel?' he asked, half doctor, half friend, for he had known her and her husband many years and they were long since on Christian name terms.

The woman turned her head restlessly on the pillows.

'I suppose I always worry . . . a bit . . . about Jackie!'

'But, my dear, you have no cause to do so. I've told you a hundred times that the boy is fit and happy . . . probably far happier than children of his age who are mentally normal. It is no great hardship to remain a child all one's life, you know . . . most five-year-olds live in a comparative heaven. It is only as we grow older that life becomes difficult for us.'

'But because he is so young in mind, his ups and downs are much more acute!' the boy's mother argued. 'Little things which are unimportant to us mean so much to him. Jackie is so hopelessly dependent . . . but NOT on me.'

'But, my dear, that is more than wise of you, surely. There is nothing worse than a child tied helplessly to its mother's apron strings. It's bad for the child and the mother.'

'So I always believed!' Mrs. Bradbourne said fiercely. 'Now I'm not so sure . . . for who else in the whole world is willing to sacrifice anything . . . anything at all, for one human being?'

'No one should sacrifice *everything* for one human being!' Dr. Law said sagely, although he could not quite follow the trend of her thought.

'Something *is* worrying you, Ethel. Won't you tell me?'

For a long moment, she hesitated. The longing to confide was intense and she was more than ready to admit that it could well be her anxious state of mind that had brought about this terrible migraine. Yet could even Jack Law understand what lay in her heart? Would he not take Mary's side just as Tom would if she were to tell him? Already the doctor had admitted that he thought it wrong even for a mother to sacrifice too much for her child's happiness.

She turned her head restlessly.

'No, there's nothing in particular, Jack. But sometimes I start worrying about Jackie's future. What will happen to him if and when I die? Who will look after him then?'

'But, my dear, there will always be Mary. She is as devoted as you are to the boy. I often think how wonderfully kind Fate has been to send Mary to you. It has been the saving of you, the making of Jackie, and she herself has grown up so charmingly.'

'But she *is* growing up!' The words burst through her lips involuntarily. 'One day she will marry and leave us.'

'Well, naturally, Ethel, but I am equally confident that her love and care for Jackie will never cease.'

'She'll have a home of her own, a husband, to care for. What time will there be for Jackie? She'll probably have . . . children . . .'

The doctor studied her tortured face and began to guess a little of what lay behind her troubled mind.

'Ethel!' he said firmly. 'You must keep a sense of proportion about your child. You have always been so sensible and I have admired you so much. You must know in your own heart what a sweet, generous and unselfish girl your Mary is. She will never walk out of Jackie's life. If she does marry, children won't come right away, will they? The weaning of her time and attention from Jackie will come about gradually. If you are wise and sensible the way you handle such an event, you can slowly accustom him to someone else . . . yourself if you feel up to it, although I believe Jackie is happier in the care of someone younger. You've said so yourself.'

Ethel Bradbourne made no reply. She had guessed he could not understand . . . that he would side with Mary. How wrong she had been ever to let Mary take such a responsible part in her child's happiness . . . how *short-sighted* of her! Now it was too late . . . Jackie would never accept a strange girl in Mary's place. It would make him ill . . . perhaps cause one of those fits she so dreaded when she could no longer convince herself that he *was* almost normal. When the fits came on him, they terrified her and even her mother's instinct could not quite obscure her horror and fright. It was always Mary who calmed the child down . . . brought him back to his 'right' mind again. There was something in Mary that had a magic power over Jackie . . . she was convinced of it. It did not occur to her that it was simply that Jackie was used to Mary, loved and trusted her, and that she had no fear of him even when he was at his more violent. Any well-trained nurse could have done the same . . . might do the same . . . if she were given time or the chance.

Ethel Bradbourne was not better by the Saturday and Mary felt it her duty to cancel her visit to the cinema with Paul, even while her Uncle advised her to go.

Paul was desperately disappointed when she spoke to him on the telephone . . . and a little angry, too. He was not by any means convinced that Mary's Aunt was not fabricating this migraine. He even went so far as to question Dr. Law, who assured him she was ill. Unhappily, he sat down to write Mary a letter . . . the first love letter he had ever written and the first Mary had ever received.

'Darling,

Promise me that you won't let anything prevent your coming home with me at the New Year? I can bear not seeing you this evening or even until Christmas if I am absolutely certain that we will have those three days, come what may.

I know this might prove a difficult promise for you to keep, but please, darling, please promise me. I want so much for you to meet my family and for them to meet you, and while I am anxious not to hurry or worry you, I am praying that you will let me give you an engagement ring and announce our engagement after that visit.

I love you, Mary . . . I say it to you in the cold, rather sobering chill of the empty surgery in which I sit so that you will know that it is not just the moonlight and the stars in your eyes that make me say something I don't really mean. I love you. And I am afraid because I can't fully believe yet that you love me. Suppose something came between us so that I lost you! I don't think my life would mean a row of pins to me if I did.

I realize that you may well be uncertain of your feelings for me . . . that you are still 'growing up' in so far as love is concerned. I'll be patient . . . wait as long as you wish for you to become my wife, so long as I am certain that you do love me; that the day will come when I can make you my own.

When shall I see you again, my own sweet Mary? When shall I see that lovely smile in your eyes and hear your soft voice, sweeter to me than anything else in the world. I never knew that love could mean just this . . . this aching to be with you, to be able to see and hear and perhaps to touch you.

I love you, now, and always, darling!

Paul.'

Mary read and re-read the letter until she knew every treasured word of it by heart. She stole away to the privacy of her own bedroom to sit down and write her reply, but somehow her pen remained unmoving. Could she, after all, make the promise Paul asked of her? Suppose her Aunt became seriously ill? Suppose Jackie had one of his fits and she really could not in all good conscience go away? She must not promise if she might have to break her word.

After a tortured half-hour of thought, she decided to make no reference to that promise . . . only to reassure him of her love for him, her longing to be with him, which she believed to be every bit as acute as his longing for her.

' . . . I look forward to meeting your family so very much,' she wrote carefully . . . 'and to wearing your ring, Paul darling. How strange it seems to be writing those words and yet how true they are. You are my darling, my heart, my whole life now and I think of you day and night and long to be with you.

Please try to understand that I couldn't go out with you yesterday. My Aunt really wasn't well and it seemed so selfish for me to leave her and go out to enjoy myself. Your disappointment cannot have been greater than mine, but I know that your unselfishness and generosity would bear me out that we should not take our happiness regardless of others. Does that sound very priggish? It is not meant to be. It's just that I should have worried and had things on my conscience and we would not have had a happy evening under those circumstances.

Maybe we can arrange to be together one evening next week. I'm sure my Aunt will be better by then, so, darling, will you ring me? I long to hear your voice.

Thank you for being patient with me. I am not as free as you are, Paul, because I owe so much to my Aunt for all she has done for me and I know you understand that. Don't ever be jealous, dearest Paul, for I love you more than anything in the world and no one shall ever part us if you don't wish it.

I love you, now and always, too!

Mary.'

Her letter thrilled and delighted him even while those uneasy qualms returned. He knew he need not really doubt her love or its enduring quality ... she was utterly sincere and her sweet, natural way of writing had convinced him. But there were those other words she had spoken equally sincerely ... 'I owe so much to my Aunt ... I am not as free as you are.' Would she ever think of herself as free ... free from gratitude and dependence on her? Was it enough that she had said she longed to wear his ring? Did she realize that if she became his wife, she must leave her old life behind her and live for and with him?

His thoughts were not selfish. He would willingly agree to her visiting her home as often as she wished, to seeing the boy and having him to stay in their home if she desired it. But she must break the ties between herself and her Aunt . . . the feeling of debt and loyalty that gave the older woman the right to expect a return. Maybe it was not Mary who must be made to realize this *but Mrs. Bradbourne.*

Mary had made no promise about the New Year. Had her omission been intentional or had she meant as much by telling him she looked forward so much to the visit? Well, there were still six weeks to go . . . time enough to extract that promise. He would try to be patient.

Mary, too, was having to exert patience. Her Aunt was extremely irritable and trying when at last the migraine left her and she was up and about again. Mary felt that an invisible barrier had been put between them by her Aunt and all their former companionship and intimacy was gone. Because of this, she was unable to voice the nagging worry that lay so close to her heart . . . her concern about Jackie's future.

Once she nearly spoke of it to her Aunt and Uncle, but some strange inner compulsion prevented her doing so, and she was still too newly in love with Paul to make her emotions public. She did not want them to know . . . not just yet.

So the days to Christmas passed, on winged feet when she was with Paul, at snail's pace when she did not see him. Her happiness became dependent upon their next meeting, the times he kissed her, phoned her, wrote to her.

Every day she fell a little more hopelessly in love with him and a little more unwilling to broach even the thought of Jackie's happiness. Whenever such thoughts threatened her, she would deliberately put them from her mind and turn her attention to some physical task, or to re-reading Paul's letters to her.

She was as patient and loving as ever with the boy. It never occurred to her to be different. She loved him deeply and her time spent with him was never a trial to her . . . it pleased her to do things for him, even when he was moody or difficult or over-demanding. He was so familiar to her as to be part of life and she had never lost her youthful, unquestioning acceptance of Fate and unqualified devotion. But she was sufficiently intelligent to accept that no man could be expected to wait indefinitely for the woman he loved . . . nor was it right to ask him to do so when the circumstances surrounding any delay could not alter. But these convictions she had buried deep down within her and she tried to think only of the immediate future, of Paul, and the New Year visit to his home.

6

Christmas came at last and Paul left for his home on Christmas Eve. He had seen Mary during the afternoon for a few minutes just to reaffirm the arrangements for her to travel down on the thirtieth, and to give her a gaily wrapped paper parcel.

Mary, too, had a present for Paul, which she gave to him, and they each promised not to look inside till the following morning. Her present to him had been a torch pen which she felt might be useful to him since he so often had to work at night and might need to jot down something important in his car. Her Uncle gave her a regular allowance so she had not had to ask for money to buy her present. If the pen was not particularly expensive, it was because she had saved all she could towards the engagement present she wished to buy him . . . a silver cigarette case. Unusually superstitious, she had not yet bought it, for it seemed to her tempting Fate to do so before he had formally asked her to marry him and she wore his ring.

Paul's gift to her was very extravagant. He had chosen the most beautiful crocodile leather handbag and in it put a large bottle of 'Toujour l'Amour' . . . her favourite perfume. There was a letter, too, which she valued almost as much as his gift, saying that he hoped this would be the last Christmas they need ever spend apart.

Christmas Day passed happily for her. Even her Aunt seemed to make the effort to be pleasant . . . for Jackie's sake, perhaps, since she was never irritable with Mary in front of the boy.

Jackie opened his stocking and played contentedly with his toys and most of all with the garage Mary had given him with its little row of petrol pumps. In the afternoon, the electric train his father and mother had given him was set up in the nursery by Uncle Tom, and Aunt Ethel went to rest.

Mary had always loved her Uncle, but it seemed to her now that they had only really become close friends since she had met Paul. Maybe it was that a new understanding had grown between them . . . as if he had suddenly realized that she was a young woman to whom he could talk on level terms and not a schoolgirl. He guessed about Paul, Mary thought. He teased her, but not unkindly, about her pending visit to Paul's family and even said jokingly:

'First impressions are very important, Mary. Mind you make a good one on your future in-laws!'

There was no doubt about the fact that her Uncle liked Paul. He thought he had the makings of a good doctor and he liked his personality, which he considered suitably masculine and yet charming. He could not think of any boy or man he had met in recent years whom he would have preferred as a husband for his niece. A pity Ethel didn't care for him. She seemed to have some rooted objection to him but without being able to give any cause. 'Just an instinct that he's wrong for Mary,' Ethel had said. As it was unlike his wife to have 'instincts' about people without good reason, he felt faintly uncomfortable whenever she spoke of Paul.

Frankly he was rather worried about Ethel. She did not seem to have been herself since that attack of 'flu. She frequently dissolved into tears in the privacy of her bedroom but again could give no reason for them . . . or would give no reason for them. He recalled Dr. Law's dropping a hint about 'the change of life' and its possible reactions on Ethel; and he put this queerness down to that cause.

Fortunately Mary was so radiant and happy around the house that even Ethel's gloominess could not destroy the atmosphere. No doubt that the girl was in love, and thank heaven the man she had chosen cared for her! No mooning and weeping for Mary. But then she had always been a good girl and she deserved her happiness . . . every moment of it. He wondered a little when the two young folk might decide to marry and whether he could afford to buy them a little house in the neighbourhood as a wedding present. The idea pleased him and he thought happily that they would not have to lose touch with Mary just because she was marrying. Nice for Jackie, too, to have her nearby . . . he was so fond of Mary.

He surveyed his son with his usual mixture of pity and affection. Poor little devil . . . with the rapidly growing body of a strong healthy boy . . . and a weak, childish mind. It had not mattered or shown so much when he was tiny, but as he grew bigger, the discrepancy between his appearance and his behaviour was more apparent and he thought of the future with faint stirrings of discomfort. Jackie would have been such a grand child . . . he was really nice-looking . . . and for a moment or two he thought about the pleasure he might have had but for that accident. He'd have been at prep. school now, and going on to Winchester where he had been.

'We ought to have had other children!' he thought, but Ethel had been adamant about it. It would not be fair to Jackie, she had said. Personally, he couldn't quite see it that way.

Uncle Tom's present to his wife and Mary had been a television set. They had often spoken of getting one and never done so. Now it was installed in the living room and that evening they all enjoyed the Christmas programme.

On Boxing Day, Ethel Bradbourne complained that she did not feel well again. Mary was in an agony of suspense. Suppose at this last moment when she had everything packed she could not go? For the first time, resentment touched her with uncomfortable fingers. It seemed as if her Aunt was always ill just when she, Mary, was going to enjoy herself. Of course, it wasn't fair to think that way, because her Aunt would never do anything so unkind, so horrible; but unless her Aunt was seriously ill she felt she could not bring herself to volunteer to stay at home. Her Aunt would have to ask her outright to do so.

Fortunately her Uncle, unknown to her, had spoken a few sharp words to his wife.

'At least, my dear, try to conceal you are not feeling well from Mary. You know how sensitive she is. She'll put off her holiday and at best go away with an uneasy mind.'

Without revealing her own shameful reasons, Ethel could not admit that this was exactly what she intended. She did not like to admit them even to herself, for she was not basically a hard, cruel or dishonest woman. But there was a blind spot where Jackie was concerned and her conviction that she was doing only what was right and best for her son, blinded her to the terrible harm she might be doing Mary. Her fears had slowly begun to poison her mind and the poison was to spread until there were no lengths she would not go to put an end to this affair with Paul Deal. At present, she could convince herself that she was doing no real harm. It had all happened very suddenly and Mary was inexperienced and still young. In her capacity of aunt and guardian she was acting in Mary's interest not to let Paul's suit sweep her off her feet into a hasty marriage.

But there seemed no way to prevent this visit to Paul's family. Nor could she close her eyes to the possible outcome. Paul and Mary might very well return as an engaged couple. He was no doubt only awaiting his parents' approval of Mary to ask her to marry him.

'I'm still not sure we should let her go in any case'; she essayed with difficulty to find other reasons to stop Mary even now. 'She's only twenty, Tom, and a very immature twenty. Suppose he really has no family in Devon?'

Tom looked as astounded as he felt.

'But, my dear, that's ridiculous. Have you forgotten that very charming invitation from young Deal's mother? Surely I didn't forget to show it to you? Asking our permission for Mary to come?'

She had not forgotten but she had hoped that he might have done so.

'Why, I should imagine they are the height of respectability, Ethel. The father is a G.P. and Dr. Law knows of them. Besides, young Paul is as decent a chap as you could wish to meet. I really can't think why you distrust him!' And with a certain amount of annoyance he left his wife alone to her failure.

He, himself, took Mary to the station and saw her onto the train. He kissed her soundly on both cheeks and told her to have a good time. As he waved good-bye, he thought how exceedingly pretty she looked in that fur-tipped hat framing her flushed face and large eyes. There was a young chap in the carriage with her who had stolen a glance or two in her direction and he chuckled to himself to think that *he* wouldn't get very far. Mary's heart had been captured already, and if he knew his niece, it wouldn't lightly change hands.

★ ★ ★

It was four o'clock when the train drew into the little country station and Mary climbed down onto the platform. The skies were heavy with dark clouds . . . perhaps snow, her travelling companions had suggested, and it was nearly dark. As she bent to lift her suitcase, she felt two strong arms go round her, and a moment later Paul was kissing her as if there were no one else alive in the world but them.

'Oh, darling, darling!' he told her, half serious, half laughing. 'I couldn't make myself believe you would be here until I saw you with my own eyes. When I saw the train coming in, I couldn't bear to look . . . just in case you hadn't come after all. *Darling!*' and he kissed her again although the train had long since drawn out and they were alone now on the deserted platform except for the porter, who watched them with a countryman's curious stare.

Mary nearly told him that she had missed the train . . . that her Aunt was ill again with the migraine and only Uncle Tom's persuasion had got her here after all. He had refused to countenance her offer to remain at home and all but bullied her to the station when the time came. But she did not want to spoil this wonderful welcome from Paul, and in any event had forgotten everything else in her life but that she was in his arms. His face was cold from the chill air but his kisses seemed to set fire to her own body and joy flooded through her, pure and unclouded. She raised a gloved finger to touch his cheek and said half smiling:

'Oh, *Paul*!'

His eyes shone back at her and he slipped his arm through hers and, taking her suitcase, walked her swiftly towards his car.

'The whole family wanted to come to meet you,' he told her as he helped her in. 'But I was too afraid you might not be there and they would see my despair. Of course, they know I'm hopelessly in love and they have all been teasing me unmercifully. They say I bring your name into every conversation and that I'm like a lovesick schoolboy.'

'Oh, dear!' Mary said, half fearfully. 'I hope they aren't expecting anything very much of me. I'm so very ordinary and dull for someone like you, Paul!' She could never quite get over her surprise that anyone as good-looking, as charming and lovable as Paul should have fallen in love with her.

'Not in the least ordinary,' Paul said firmly, 'and never never dull. You're such a wonderful girl, Mary, and always a surprise to me. I can't bring myself to believe in my good fortune that *you* should love *me*.'

'Perhaps all lovers feel this inadequacy when they measure themselves against the man or woman they love,' Mary said dreamily. 'Paul, talk to me! I'm frightened of your family.'

But he only drove a little faster, laughing gaily like a young boy, so happy and confident did he feel. He longed now to open the front door and be able to show her off to his family . . . to say, 'Well, here she is!' and see their reactions to her. They were all at home except his young brother who was unable to get leave from the hospital. But Paul was unashamedly glad about this. Neal was confoundedly attractive and he didn't want any competition for his girl.

'My girl!' he said, touching her hand gently. 'Tell me it's true, Mary.'

'Yes, I'm your girl!' she answered him shyly.

Ten minutes later, Paul was opening the front door and it seemed to Mary as if a hundred people were greeting her and at least a dozen young children were crowding round her all talking at once.

But Paul just shouldered his way through them with an elder brother's unconcern and took Mary straight to his mother and father.

'Here she is!' he told them proudly.

Mary held out her hand but suddenly found herself being kissed by Paul's mother and returning this warm greeting.

'We're so glad to have you, Mary dear! Paul has been worried sick you might not come. Now you're here and he is happy at last!'

'Let me introduce the family to you,' said Paul's father as the crowd pressed about her once more. 'First Jean, the eldest girl!'

'Hullo, Mary, and Happy Christmas!'

Mary found herself looking into a face not unlike Paul's except for the fact that it was wholly feminine and lacking Paul's firmness of jaw. Although Jean was wearing slacks and a jersey, she nevertheless had contrived to look very fashionable, for the trousers were 'drain-pipe' and the brilliant emerald-green jersey fisherman's knit. Her lipstick was cherry red and Paul's violet blue eyes looked into Mary's merrily.

Mary found it hard to believe that this girl was only two years older than herself. She felt instinctively that she was far older in every way.

'And this is Neal . . . the future surgeon of the family!'

They shook hands and Mary thought that twenty-year-old Neal, while being quite unlike Paul, was nevertheless nice-looking. He had his mother's fair hair and hazel eyes. Jean and Paul were like their father. So he had got leave after all.

The next sister, Margaret, was seventeen and Mary instantly felt a liking for the young girl for she was very shy and blushed when she said hullo to Mary. Because she had herself always been shy and awkward with strangers, Mary could sympathize and she said quickly:

'I'm sure we shall be good friends!' and the girl gave a sweet smile in reply.

The two youngsters, twelve and ten, were anything but shy. Jonathon and Joan were typical of any healthy rowdy boy and girl and it wasn't long before they were teasing her about Paul as often as they teased him about Mary.

It was Mary's first introduction into the life of a large family and although she felt a little overcome at first, Paul was always at her side and she soon found herself growing accustomed to the noise and orderly confusion! Tea was a real family affair with large brown eggs for those who were hungry and an enormous pile of Scotch pancakes which, to Mary's amazement, soon disappeared. Everyone laughed and talked, interrupting themselves and other people's conversation, and she contrasted this friendly informal meal with their own quiet repasts at home.

Occasionally she would turn her head to find Paul's eyes on her face and she longed suddenly to be alone with him so that she could tell him how much she was enjoying this and how nice she thought his family were. His mother and father she found particularly charming. The old doctor was round and dumpy with a shock of grey hair and twinkling blue eyes. He seemed quite immune to the noise until the phone rang and then silence fell instantly and Mary realized with a little shock of surprise that this was, for all its family life, essentially a doctor's house and that they had been trained from infancy to be quiet when the phone rang, and no doubt at surgery times or when a patient called. In between whiles they could make as much noise as they pleased.

A moment later, Dr. Deal came back into the dining-room with his hat and coat and announced that he might be late back.

'Think it might be an appendix,' he informed them. 'Like to come along, Neal, and help diagnose?'

The young medical student jumped

to his feet and Mary wondered if Paul would have gone if she had not been here. But guessing her thoughts, he said:

'The poor patient would think he was dying if three of us turned up. Besides, Neal needs some practise!'

Neal gave him a playful push and then he and his father were gone. Instantly, the noise broke out again until Mrs. Deal gave the order to clear the table.

Everyone helped . . . that is to say, everyone but Paul and Mary.

Mrs. Deal refused Mary's offer with a smile.

'Another of our rules, Mary. Guests and their host or hostess are excused domestic chores.'

'But I'd rather you didn't think of me as a guest!' Mary said spontaneously, and immediately blushed as she realized the implication of her words. In a moment, the two younger children noticed and remarked on it and it was the shy Margaret who dragged them away to the kitchen reproving them for their bad manners.

For a few moments, she and Paul were alone in the large drawing-room with its big log fire and bright Christmas holly and decorations. Paul put his arm around her shoulders and she leant back contentedly, closing her eyes.

'I'm so glad I came, Paul. I'm loving every moment of it!' she told him. 'Your family are all so nice!'

'I like them!' Paul laughed. 'And they like you, Mary. They have already accepted you, even though Mother wouldn't let you wash up!' A little unkindly he had purposefully brought the rosy colour back to her cheeks. 'Darling, I think I love you most when you are so shy and blush . . . just as Margaret does.'

'How do you know they have accepted me?' Mary asked.

'Because they are all being themselves. If they had been quiet and well behaved and polite, it would have meant they hoped you wouldn't come again!'

He bent his head and touched his lips to her hair. 'Darling, thank you for my pen. I use it at night to write romantic sonnets to you!'

'Silly!' Mary laughed at him, thanking him in her turn for the bag which she had carried today. He had already noticed that she wore his perfume.

'They're not such a bad lot really!' Paul said, referring to his brothers and sisters again. 'You'll see this evening how tactful they will be. At about ten-thirty they will all say they are tired and retire self-consciously to bed. I heard Mother briefing them yesterday! You see, you're the first romance we've had in the family so they aren't well trained!'

'Oh, Paul!' Mary smiled. 'How wonderful it all is. I'm so terribly happy.'

Her happiness radiated from her throughout the rest of the evening. She played noisy card games with the younger children and 'Scrabble' with Paul and Margaret and Jean. Watching her from the armchair where she was knitting, Mrs. Deal knew herself to be quite content with her son's choice. She knew Paul would not have asked Mary home had he not intended to marry her . . . at least, not during the Christmas festivities which were and always had been kept exclusively a family affair. And when he had asked her to write a note to Mary's Uncle and Aunt, she had been doubly sure of his intentions. And she was glad now that it had happened. There was a quality of sweetness about Mary that weighed far more importantly with her than her prettiness or her nice manners or even her delightful way with the children. She felt instinctively that Mary would make the right companion for her Paul . . . and no one could possibly fail to notice that she was head over heels in love with him.

She sighed, wondering if life could really hold so much happiness in store for one woman and ask nothing in return. For her life had been perfect. She had never ceased to love Paul's father; they had six healthy, happy and good children. They had never lacked the necessities of life even while they may not have had any luxuries. Could she dare hope that her other five children, all as dear to her in their separate ways as Paul, would make as good a choice and find their love returned?

Well, Paul was setting them all a good example and they were all good, nice people, her children. They, like Paul, would find someone worthy of them, too.

She stood up and put away her knitting and called the two elder girls to help her in the kitchen while the boys were instructed to tidy up. Mary went upstairs to unpack and tried not to think that only two days hence she must pack again and go home.

7

As Paul had said they would, the entire family departed in varying little groups at half past ten. Had Paul not pre-warned her, Mary would not have realized they were deliberately leaving her and Paul the chance to be alone together. Now as the door closed behind Paul's father, who had stayed for a few minutes longer for a 'night-cap', she turned and smiled at the man beside her.

'Quite a tactical operation!' he grinned.

'Paul, they're so nice, all of them!' Mary cried from her heart. 'I don't know whom I like the most. Your father is a darling, although I suspect that beneath his jovial easy-going air he can be very thoughtful!'

'And authoritative!' Paul added with a grimace. 'There was no nonsense allowed when we were all youngsters. If we cheeked Mother or did something particularly outrageous, we got the cane . . . good old-fashioned punishment which we never resented, even when we left the room with stinging backsides!'

Mary laughed with him.

'And your mother, Paul . . . she's a dear. And so wonderfully happy. It pleases her to serve those she loves.'

'I think *you* are very like her!' Paul remarked more seriously. 'I hadn't thought of it until now, but maybe that is one of the reasons I fell in love with you. Mary, you are going to marry me? I don't think I could bear it if you said 'no'.'

Mary did not think she could bear to disappoint him and as she hesitated she saw all the colour drain from his face. She sought the right words.

'Paul, don't hurry me too much. It isn't that I'm not sure that I want to marry you. I do . . . just as much as you want to marry me. But things are so perfect right now that I'd like to . . . to stay as we are for a while. Can you understand that?'

Paul bit his lip.

'You mean, you don't even want my ring to wear?'

The pain in his voice tore at her heart. Swiftly she held out her hands to him and said:

'Yes, yes, of course I want to be engaged, Paul darling. It's just that I . . . I don't want to get married yet . . . not for a while.' Not until I am sure Jackie will be all right, she said to herself, but could not bring herself to say to him. Clearly no such thought had crossed his mind and he might not understand how greatly Jackie needed her.

Paul's face was glowing again. He looked relieved and happy, believing her hesitation to be a natural part of her make-up. This was her first introduction to love . . . and being loved. She was happy and content that they should belong simply as an engaged couple. He could not expect her to have the same urgent physical desires as he had himself ... the same longing for complete possession. She was newly awakened to love and he respected her innocence and the purity of her mind. Deep down within her, he knew there were fires to burn as brightly as his own and there would be many years in the future when they could give each other that part of their love, too. He would not let her see anything of his own impatience; of the heights of longing which tortured him when she was in his arms. He was many years older than she was and it was up to him to give her all the time she needed. He would not rush her into a quick wedding if she did not wish it, too.

Even as he drew her into his arms and showered kisses on her face and throat and hair, he believed her to be only a little moved by their joint emotion. He could not know that Mary had to strive almost as hard as he was doing not to abandon herself completely and utterly to the wild tumult of her own desires. Paul had been wrong to suppose that she was unawakened yet. With every kiss and each embrace, she knew her longing for him to be almost unbearable, so that she would draw away from him and he would believe that he had frightened her and grow calm and tender and bring a smile back to her eyes.

How precious were those moments alone together on the deep sofa in front of the blazing fire. Paul had turned off the big centre light and only a lamp glowed in the far corner of the room. After a little while, they leaned back, arms and hands entwined, eyes staring into each other's faces.

'I hope our home will be like this!' Mary said dreamily, allowing herself to dream that she could soon leave Jackie and marriage to Paul could and would come true.

'It will be exactly as you want it, my darling . . . everything will always be just as you want it.'

'You mean you would even stay with

me if some patient wanted you in the middle of the night and I preferred you not to go?' Mary teased him. Then seeing his stricken face, said quickly: 'Paul, I know a doctor is dedicated to his work . . . that it must come first before anything else, even a wife. I wouldn't want it any different, darling Paul!'

He gripped her hands more tightly and sighed:

'I don't think it is so easy after all to be a good doctor and a good husband. I shall be late back to meals, or not back at all. I may not be able to go out if we've planned an evening, or not turn up if we have a party.'

'As if any of those things matter so long as you love me!' Mary told him. 'I wouldn't mind them, Paul, any more than your mother has minded.'

Paul grimaced.

'It's odd you should say that. Mother was talking to me about it last night. She said it hadn't been easy when she was first married . . . that it had taken time to adjust herself to second place and second best. She said: 'If real love exists between you and the girl you marry, Paul, then you will both be happy. But make sure it is real . . . to both of you!' '

'It's real to me!' Mary whispered. 'The most important, real and wonderful thing that has ever happened to me. I can't imagine now how I can have lived contentedly through twenty years without knowing and loving you.'

'And I've thought the same,' Paul agreed, 'although I have lived through thirty years, or nearly. Mary, you don't think those nine years between our ages matter?'

'How could they matter?' Mary answered. 'We love each other . . . that's the only thing in the world that matters.'

Paul stood up abruptly and walked over to the walnut desk that stood in a corner of the room. A moment later he was back and lifted Mary's left hand in his own. He slipped the ring over her third finger and said:

'I have had *Paul and Mary* inscribed in it! Do you like it, dearest?'

Mary gazed down at her finger and her heart beat furiously with mingled emotions as she saw the beautiful sapphire and diamond stones, set beautifully in a platinum twist. Paul's engagement ring. Now, if she accepted it, she would be his fiancée. They were engaged to be married.

She could not bear to refuse it.

'Don't you like it, Mary? Or is it that you don't want it?'

She jumped up and threw herself into his arms. He felt the tears coursing down her cheeks and heard the soft broken sobs that came from her throat.

'Mary, darling Mary, you mustn't cry. Tell me, dear heart, tell me what's the matter?'

'It's just that . . . that I'm so happy . . . so happy!' Mary whispered. 'It makes me afraid . . . '

'You must never be afraid with me!' Paul told her firmly as he tilted back her head and tried to dry the tears that still ran down her cheeks. 'I don't know what it is you fear but if it has to do with us, then forget all about it. We are going to be the happiest couple in the whole world . . . happier even than Mother and Father have been, and we shall have eight children instead of six if that's what *you* want. Mary, stop crying, my love, please. It breaks my heart to see you weep.'

Gradually she controlled herself and a new calm replaced her momentary panic. Paul was right . . . she must not be afraid. She had been a coward until now and the Fates were never kind to cowards. When she returned home, she would talk to her Aunt about Jackie and come to some happy arrangement for his future. She ought to have done so weeks ago . . . certainly before she had allowed Paul to believe she would marry him in the foreseeable future, when it might be years before she could leave her little cousin. She had been weak in refusing to face this fact. Now the force of her love for Paul was making her strong.

Then all coherent thought ceased as Paul took her into his arms and began again to kiss her. She was not unaware of the constraint he put upon himself as the moments passed, for she was herself as keyed up and aroused in her emotions as he was. Their kisses became wilder and less controlled and Mary knew real temptation for the first time in her life. Suppose she were to give herself to Paul now . . . here in this firelit room where they seemed alone in the whole world. It would be so easy . . . so wonderful . . . so absolutely right . . . and she might never have that chance again. To possess and be possessed in the great height of real love. It could not be wrong! Yet even as she voiced to herself those words, *she knew that it would be wrong.* Paul might lose a little of his respect for her, she for herself; and they would both be abusing the trust his parents obviously placed in them both.

But it was Paul who drew away from her first. He was breathing deeply and his voice was hoarse as he said:

'Mary, don't let's wait too long to be married . . . I want you so!'

'And I want you, too, Paul!' Mary told him without shyness now, for she was too deeply involved to be aware of herself. 'In the spring, Paul . . . *if everything is all right* . . . I'll marry you in the spring.'

It was sooner than he had dared to hope and he was so full of eagerness, gratitude, plans, that he did not take in her qualification. Carried away by his happiness and enthusiasm, Mary allowed herself to dream with him. It was only when the old grandfather clock in the hall struck midnight that they realized how time had sped.

'The hour for my Cinderella to retire!' Paul smiled as he spoke. 'But Prince Charming is nevertheless distinctly hungry. Let's raid the larder!'

She followed him out to the kitchen and Paul rummaged in the fridge and larder and produced some cold pie and a plate of apples and bananas. Next he found a jug of coffee which he proceeded with great efficiency to heat with some milk. They sat down to their meal, laughing like two school-children. They looked nearly as guilty when they heard footsteps in the hall and saw someone opening the kitchen door.

It was Paul's father.

'Well, well, well!' he said, smiling at them both. 'And I thought you were burglars!'

'Dad, what a fib!' Paul chaffed his father. 'You heard the chink of plates and saucepans and wanted to join in the fun.'

'Cheeky young devil, isn't he?' old Dr. Deal said to Mary as he cut himself a large slice of the pie. 'Always was.'

'I'm glad you've come down, Dad!' Paul said, grinning. 'You can be the first to congratulate us.'

The old man's eyes twinkled and went directly to Mary's hand where Paul's ring sparkled.

'This is a surprise!' he said in mock tones. 'My heartiest good wishes to you both, and would one of you kindly pour me a cup of coffee.'

'I've a mind to raid the cellar and open a bottle!' Paul said. 'Then you could drink a toast to us both. You can't do it in coffee, Dad. It has to be spirits.'

'We'll open the bottle tomorrow,' his father said firmly, 'when the others can join in. Why, your Mother would never forgive me . . . or you, if she thinks I've been told the news before her. I shall have to be surprised all over again at breakfast!'

Then he grew serious for a moment as he reached over and patted Mary's hand.

'Paul's a lucky fellow. To be quite honest, Mother and I knew he was going to ask you, so we guessed it might happen. But we hadn't met you then. Now we know you, we are really happy about it, my dear.'

Mary stood up and with one of her

spontaneous gestures which always so enchanted Paul, she kissed his father on top of his grey head.

'I'll try always to make him happy! I'll only ever do what is best for Paul.'

The old man patted her hand again and said gruffly:

'Don't be too unselfish, Mary. You remind me of my wife, Paul's mother. It doesn't do to think too much of others. We men are only human and sometimes it's tempting to take advantage of so much unselfishness and generosity . . . and then we hate ourselves.' He coughed as if his own words had embarrassed him. Then his eyes began to twinkle and his voice was normal as he said:

'See if there's any top of the milk in the fridge, Paul. I could just do with a banana and cream!'

★　★　★

It was the last day of the year and the happiest day Mary could remember.

She had slept until nine-thirty in a deep contented fashion so that she awoke utterly refreshed and her eyes and face glowing.

As she made her way downstairs, she was greeted by what seemed to her to be a hundred voices talking at once. Paul's brothers and sisters all wanted to see her ring and shyly she held out her hand.

'Congratulations, Mary . . . or I should congratulate Paul, lucky chap!' Neal's voice.

'It'll give a wonderful zip to the party tonight . . . Paul timed it nicely!' Jean's friendly tones.

'Oh, Mary, how beautiful . . . it's almost as pretty as you are!' followed by Margaret's shy blush.

'Golly, he must love her!' That was young Jonathon. From his sister there was just a drawn-out 'Coo!'

They were shaking her hand and slapping her on the back and Mary was glad when Paul's voice said firmly:

'Will you kindly all unhand my

fiancée so that I can kiss her good morning!'

And he proceeded to do so in front of them all and quite unheeding of their good-natured chaffing. Mary knew she was blushing but she did not care.

Then Paul took her through to the kitchen where his mother was making fresh coffee and there were just the three of them. Mrs. Deal opened her arms and quite simply enfolded Mary, saying:

'I'm so glad for Paul. We're all so pleased!'

Dropping a kiss on top of Mary's head, Paul went out and left them alone.

'I'll try so hard to make him happy!' Mary promised. 'Please believe me!'

'My dear child, you don't have to try. You make him happy just by being what you are . . . and because you love him. I hope your Aunt and Uncle will be pleased about this, too?'

Mary quickly dropped her eyes and walked over to the window, staring out across the barrenness of a winter garden.

Would Uncle Tom and Aunt Ethel be pleased? Her Uncle, yes, but what about her Aunt? She had given no indication that she liked Paul . . . *on the contrary*, and instinct told her that her Aunt would oppose her marriage, though on what basis Mary could not imagine, unless she believed it to be Mary's duty to sacrifice her love and Paul's for the helpless little boy. Yet surely she could *not* expect it.

To cover her own uneasy thoughts, she said quickly:

'My Uncle likes Paul very much indeed; I think he knew Paul was going to . . . to propose to me. I think he'll be very happy.'

'And your Aunt?' the soft voice questioned her.

'Well, my Aunt told me she thought nine years was rather a big difference in our ages.' Mary improvised the alternative excuse readily. 'But my Uncle is many years older than she is so I don't think she can exactly object on those grounds.'

'Maybe your Aunt feels you are young yet to settle down!' Paul's mother suggested shrewdly. 'Paul tells me you have always been very much a 'home girl'. It's possible your Aunt thinks you should see more of the world and other men before making your final choice.'

Mary's eyes shone with sudden hope. Perhaps that was the reason. Maybe she had entirely misjudged her Aunt's motives and that she was only trying to protect Mary from a possible mistake.

'Perhaps it *is* that!' she admitted happily. 'All the same, I *am* quite sure about Paul. I know I'll never love anyone but him, however many men I meet.'

'We all think that the first time we fall in love!' Mrs. Deal smiled. 'Our Jean has already been in and out of love three times and each time it is supposed to be the 'real' thing.'

'But I do know it . . . deep down

143

inside!' Mary argued in defence of her love. 'Please don't doubt it, Mrs. Deal.'

The older woman's eyes studied the girl for a long moment and then she said softly:

'No, I don't doubt it, Mary . . . not from you. You and Jean are very different. I think you are more like my Margaret. She will fall in love once . . . and I hope and pray that love may be returned. Jean could always adapt herself to someone else . . . even to second best, but Margaret, never. Her emotions go too deep.'

She beckoned to Mary to sit down at the table and eat the breakfast she had prepared. Mary found herself ravenous and as she ate, apologized for not being down in time for the family breakfast. Mrs. Deal assured her that they had let her lie in deliberately and that the younger children had been threatened with no party tonight if they woke her up.

'Otherwise you would never have had a wink after seven a.m.'

'I think the children are all so nice!' Mary said shyly. 'What fun for Paul to grow up in a large family.'

'You have no brothers or sisters?'

'My parents died when I was still tiny and I was brought up by my Uncle and Aunt.' She hesitated for a second and then added: 'They have one child, my cousin Jackie. He's ten.'

'Yes, I remember now that Paul wrote and told me about him. He hasn't been very well?'

'He has always been quite strong physically but he is mentally backward!' Mary said. 'He is as dear to me as my own brother and it will not be easy for me to leave him when . . . when I marry Paul!'

Mrs. Deal was silent. Paul had not told her that there was anything the matter with the little boy's brain. Had he deliberately refrained from doing so or had he not considered it of any import? Perhaps it wasn't important. After all, the child was not Mary's brother, and maybe the instability had

145

been caused by illness or an accident.

She was not a narrow-minded woman and her very nature made her kind and full of pity, which she took care not to show to those less fortunate than herself. Yet she sincerely hoped there was no hereditary disease that might pass on to Paul's children. Well, he was a doctor and quite old enough to make his own decisions. He had no doubt seen the child and attended him in a medical capacity, so he would have the details at his finger-tips. He had probably already ascertained that the child's disease was not of a hereditary nature. Or if it was, he loved the girl too much to let anything stand in the way of his marriage to her. He was old enough to make his own decisions and it was not her policy to interfere or ask questions.

'Perhaps you could bring your little cousin down here some time to visit us?' she suggested kindly. 'I know the children would do their best to keep him entertained and amused.'

146

Mary's eyes shone.

'How kind of you to suggest it. Jackie has never been away from home in his life. Perhaps my Aunt and Uncle would not let him come . . . but maybe if Dr. Law says it is all right —'

'Mum!'

Jonathon's young voice broke in on their conversation. 'Paul says we must have some french chalk to put on the floor if we're going to dance and Joan and me'll go down to the village on our bikes if that's all right.'

'Well, mind the traffic on the main road!' Mrs. Deal said. Two moments later, Margaret appeared with an armful of flowers which she told them Edwin Hutchin had brought down from the Grange. Edwin was Jean's new boy-friend and the younger son of the local 'squire'. He was coming to the party tonight.

'Will you help me arrange them, Mary? No one else seems to have time and I'm not very good at flower decoration.'

The rest of the morning passed swiftly, as they prepared the big sitting-room for the New Year Party. The boys took most of the furniture to other rooms, leaving only a few comfortable chairs for the older people who would want to sit. Great logs were carried in by Paul and Neal and stacked either side of the big farmhouse fireplace.

Coming in at lunch-time, Dr. Deal remarked that it was one advantage of having a big family . . . there were plenty of people to do the work.

After lunch, Mary, Jean and Margaret helped Mrs. Deal prepare the buffet supper. The general air of excitement increased and after a tea consisting of buffet pieces that were rejected as 'not good enough' to display later, the two younger children were sent off to rest and Mrs. Deal also went to lie down. Mary, Paul, Neal and Margaret played 'Scrabble' to fill in the hour before it was time to dress and Jean stayed in the kitchen to iron her dress.

It amazed Mary that the entire family should actually have managed to assemble on time, such had been the scramble for the bathroom, the anxious cries from the girls to borrow a pin or button a dress, and from the boys for someone else to tie their bow ties. Mary had been left in comparative peace except for a brief visit from Jean in a glorious shimmering dance dress which, together with her brushed-up hairstyle, had transformed her into someone quite different.

'You look lovely!' Mary told her. 'But much older!'

Jean smiled mischievously.

'Well, Edwin likes sophisticated women,' she said calmly. 'And I'm just a little in love with Edwin . . . maybe one day I'll marry him.'

'Oh, Jean, has he asked you?'

Jean laughed again.

'No! But he would if I gave him the chance. I prefer to keep him at arm's length for a while, figuratively speaking, of course. He kisses divinely. Mary, are you shocked? You remind me so much of Margaret. She always blushes when I say things like that!'

'No, I'm not shocked!' Mary said truthfully. 'But I can't altogether understand you. I don't think I'd want to . . . to have a man make love to me if I wasn't in love with him.'

'Nonsense!' Jean said airily. 'It can be great fun. I like men . . . and they like me, and I'm vain enough to enjoy their admiration.'

Mary did not doubt that she had plenty of it if she looked as she did tonight. By contrast, Mary felt gauche and far too youthfully dressed. When she voiced her opinion of herself, Jean instantly shook her head.

'Oh, no, Mary . . . you're just right. I thought how clever it was of you to dress to your type . . . the young, virginal touch. I might have guessed you didn't do it on purpose. You really are sweet!'

She was so obviously sincere that Mary felt she had intended a compliment.

'But I have often thought I'd like to be your type!' she told Jean. 'Self-assured and chic and clever.'

'My dear, Paul loves you because you are what you are!'

Jean spoke, as indeed she felt, as if she were years older and wiser than Mary. 'No one could help loving you, Mary. I am sure you never did an unkind deed in your life.'

'That makes me sound terribly priggish and a prude, too. It's just that I've seen so little of life compared with you, Jean, that I've never been tempted.'

'That doesn't say much for Paul as a lover!' Jean said, her eyes sparkling with merriment.

Mary blushed furiously as she remembered last evening and how she had been tempted to forget everything but her love for Paul, her need of him and his of her.

'All right!' Jean said. 'I take that back. Anyway, I didn't really mean to bring up the temptations of sex. I meant in everyday life. I'm sure you never told a lie or were unkind to anyone . . . that kind of thing.'

'Not if I can help it!' Mary admitted. 'But I don't believe you have, either, Jean. You just like to make other people think you're wicked.'

'Clever Mary!' Jean said, half laughing, half seriously. 'I'm afraid Mother's upbringing has been too thoroughly instilled into me ever to deviate very far from the paths of righteousness. All the same, it's fun to skirt around the edges. I suppose I'm a born flirt, too. You're far too honest to be a flirt.'

Again Mary felt her cheeks flame. How dishonest she had been . . . far far more so than Jean could have been in her life. She had let Paul propose to her and given him to believe she could marry him in the spring. She had not had the courage to tell him she might not be able to marry him for years.

Suddenly Jean bent over and kissed Mary lightly on the cheek.

'I'm so glad it's you Paul has chosen!'

she said softly. 'He has always been nearer and dearer to me than the others. Paul has always been home-loving and somehow we have got along fine together all our lives. Neal and I squabble most of the while . . . too near to each other in age. But Paul . . . well, he's good the way you are, Mary. We've often been afraid some scheming female would get hold of him and make him miserable. You've no idea how happy Mother and I are about you.'

'I hope you and I will always be good friends!' Mary said, returning her kiss with real feeling. 'You know that Paul and I will always welcome you to our home when we're married. You mustn't feel you're going to lose him.'

'That's just it, I don't . . . none of us do. We were talking about you at breakfast when Paul told us you were engaged. We all agreed that you were going to be 'one of us' and that once you stopped being shy with us, you'd be like a real sister instead of our brother's girl-friend . . . fiancée, I mean!'

Paul's fiancée! Mary thought as she linked arms with Jean and walked downstairs. Yes, but how long before she could be his wife?

8

The party was perhaps the most wonderful that Mary had ever been to. All the male guests clamoured for dances with Paul's girl, showering her with congratulations and compliments and making her feel the belle of the ball. During one of his dances with her, Paul told her that she was indeed the loveliest girl there.

'In that cloudy white net, you look like a bride, my darling!' he whispered as he held her close in his arms. 'Sweet seventeen . . . everything that is fresh and young and adorable!'

Excitement and Paul's extravagant remarks, together with her enjoyment of the evening, lent an additional colour to her cheeks and stars to her eyes. Catching sight of herself in a mirror as Paul whirled her round the room to a gay waltz, Mary hardly knew the glamorous, pretty girl for herself.

'Love has made me beautiful for Paul!' she told herself as she gave herself up completely to the magic of the moment.

There was little formality about the party. Each of the Deal brothers and sisters had invited two guests so that they were seventeen young people . . . not too many for the drawing-room. Jonathon managed the gramophone most efficiently and gave them a variety of records to which they could dance. At eleven o'clock they paused to tackle the buffet supper. Afterwards, Jonathon and Joan were sent to bed and the remaining fifteen young ones began to try out barn dancing. Mary knew none of the steps but Paul and her other partners were only too willing to teach her, and having a good ear for rhythm and a quick receptive mind and nimble toes she was soon able to hold her own in the Gay Gordons, the Dashing White Sergeant and the Hill Billies.

Once or twice she caught sight of

Jean, dancing more frequently with Edwin than with anyone else, but tantalizing him at the same time by laughing into the eyes of her other partners, as if she were just as interested in them.

'I'm glad you don't flirt with anyone but me!' Paul declared, following her gaze. 'I'd be terribly jealous.'

'Perhaps it would do you good!' Mary teased him. 'You'll get tired of me if you're too sure of me.'

'Never!' Paul vowed, his eyes serious. 'Don't change yourself, Mary. It's you I love . . . you as you are.'

'But I shall grow up . . . and grow old!' Mary said with a little frown.

'In years, yes. In wisdom, perhaps, but not in yourself. Mother has never lost her . . . her innocence. She trusts everyone, loves everyone, and would never believe an unkind word about another human being unless she was forced to. Even when we had burglars here and they stole practically the only valuables we had, she excused them by saying they must have been starving and in greater need of the money than we were of the objects. She cannot see badness in anyone since there is none in herself.'

'Maybe she would understand that I *cannot* marry Paul until I'm sure Jackie will be all right without me,' Mary thought. And because now she seemed so often to be spoiling every precious moment by her doubts for the future, she knew herself suddenly and strangely eager to go home. She had thought that two days here with Paul and his family would be far too short . . .

Now she must get home and straighten out her life. She must make up her mind once and for all to tackle her Aunt . . . insist that someone else should take her place.

Paul travelled back to London with her on New Year's Day and accompanied her home. She did not ask him in because, as she told him, she wanted to be able to break the news of her engagement to her Aunt and Uncle and let them get accustomed to the idea before he met them again. He had promised her not to announce it in any paper until she had their approval. Apart from anything else, she was still under twenty-one.

His good-bye kiss to her as the taxi drew up outside her home was full of confidence and happiness. Hers had something of desperation in it. Suppose they must go on living this way with these continual good-byes for years?

'I'll telephone you tomorrow!' Paul promised and then smiled ruefully. 'It isn't going to be easy parting from you, darling, after living under the same roof for two days. The time went so quickly and yet it seems as if we were together so long.'

'It was wonderful, Paul . . . everything was perfect!' Mary told him softly. 'I hope . . . I hope I can go again.'

But her last words were drowned as his lips sought hers in one last kiss, and then at last he released her and she watched the taxi drive away, a little of herself seeming to go with him.

She turned and let herself into the house.

Jackie was already in bed and she went straight to his room where her Aunt was reading to him. She greeted Mary somewhat coldly.

'Did you enjoy yourself? You look tired.'

'It's a long journey, Aunt Ethel!' Mary told her quietly. She was suddenly glad that her gloves covered Paul's ring. She did not want to break her news in front of Jackie.

She turned her attention to the boy who greeted her with a rapturous welcome. He hugged her and chattered away to her and seemed thrilled to have her back.

'He missed you terribly!' Mrs. Bradbourne said markedly. 'I told him you would be back today but he couldn't seem to understand and cried and cried.'

'Jackie wanted Mary!' the boy said. Mary's heart sank even while she wondered if he were merely imitating his mother; if he really had cried. She bit her lip and sitting down on the edge of his bed, began to tell him about the train journey.

Half an hour later, she left her small cousin fast asleep and went to her own room to tidy herself before supper. She heard her Uncle's key in the front door and his gruff voice as he called to her Aunt, and felt a little more confident. Uncle Tom would be on her side!

With a last look at the sparkling stones bravely flaunting their message on her left hand, Mary went downstairs.

Her Uncle and Aunt were drinking sherry. Having kissed his niece, he offered her a glass which, though she usually refused it, she took tonight.

'Have a good time, my dear?'

'Perfect, Uncle Tom . . . ' Shyly, she held out her hand. She saw his eyes twinkle and then he raised his glass and said:

'Congratulations, Mary. Why didn't

you bring the fellow back with you?'

'Congratulations?' Her Aunt's tone of voice was sharp and dangerously quiet. 'Upon what?'

'Paul has asked me to marry him, Aunt Ethel!' Mary said quietly, holding out her hand for the ring to be seen and praying that her Aunt would suddenly smile and be glad.

'I must say I think you've been a little . . . well, underhand, Mary. Couldn't you have waited to obtain our permission first? It's surely a question of good manners.'

Mary flushed painfully. She *would* have told her Aunt . . . asked for her blessing before she went, if she had dared bring up the question of Jackie. But her Aunt had been stiffly unapproachable and she had not dared . . .

'Nonsense, Ethel!' Uncle Tom rose to her defence. 'You knew as well as I did what was going on. Young men don't ask girls to spend some time at their homes unless their intentions are serious. I think Mary's chosen very well, myself . . . he seems to me to be a nice, steady young man and he can well afford to support her.'

'And have you also arranged a wedding date?' Her Aunt's voice was cold and unfriendly . . . sarcastic even.

'No! Paul would like me to marry him in the spring, but naturally I wanted to talk to you first. You know I wouldn't want to marry without yours and Uncle Tom's blessing. You have both always been so good to me. And you know I couldn't go . . . wouldn't . . . until Jackie was used to the idea of my being away. Aunt Ethel, you haven't anything against Paul?'

'I know very little about him!' her Aunt said shortly. 'So I don't know anything to his discredit. But I do consider you are very young to be married, Mary. You don't come of age until next June . . . and you are young for your age.'

'Then why not combine twenty-first celebrations with a wedding?' Uncle Tom suggested. 'I'm sure Mary will wait until then.'

'Are you absolutely sure you want to marry?' Mrs. Bradbourne ignored her husband's remarks. 'I have sensed an uncertainty about you, Mary. Are you sure you are not letting this first love-affair sweep you off your feet?'

For a tiny moment, Mary hesitated. She *had* doubts, but not of her love for Paul.

'I love him!' she said at last. 'I'll never change my mind about that.'

The older woman drew a deep breath as her mind leapt to meet this challenge. She turned to her husband and said:

'I think it would be a good idea if you left the two of us together . . . for a girlish gossip!' she added with a smile that never touched her eyes. Mary felt her heart sink. Was this to be the moment? She must not lack courage now . . . for Paul's sake and the sake of her love.

When her Uncle left the room, giving her a silent almost conspiratorial clap on the shoulder as he passed by her, she turned back to look her Aunt in the face. But Mrs. Bradbourne dropped her eyes quickly, unable to meet that direct clear gaze.

'Sit down, Mary!' she said.

Obediently Mary sat down, clasping her hands in front of her lap. She waited for her Aunt to speak.

'I am quite ready to believe that you are in love,' Mrs. Bradbourne picked her words with care. 'You have convinced me of that, otherwise I would not be talking to you like this. But I would not have done so had I believed you might change your mind. You see, Mary, I am thinking now not so much of you but of the man you profess means so much to you.'

Mary's hands and lips trembled.

'Please go on!'

'Have you never stopped to think about the reason for the outcome of marriage? The wedding service tells us clearly that it is for the procreation of children. Are you willing to take the risk of having children, Mary? Is Paul? Are you both content to do without?'

'I . . . I don't understand!' Mary whispered. What was her Aunt inferring? Why should she suggest it might be a risk to have children? Or go without. 'I don't understand,' she said again.

'I am speaking, of course, of Jackie, my son, and your cousin,' Mrs. Bradbourne went on inexorably. 'You are old enough now, Mary, to hear the truth. You always believed Jackie was . . . was backward because of his accident. Well, that is not so. Of course, everyone thinks so . . . just as we intended they should. At first, I thought so myself; *our doctor gave his assurances after the accident that he was in no way harmed*. But I had to be sure, and I went to nearly every specialist in London. They all asked me the same question . . . was there any history of mental disease in either my or your Uncle's family. Your Uncle was able to trace his family history back for several generations. But I was not. Your father had been dead some years and the records of our family which I believe him to have had were lost in Norway, where as you know he died. Nor was I able to trace the doctor we had had as children. So you see, I could not answer their question in the negative.'

'You mean . . . the specialists believe Jackie's trouble to be . . . to be . . . inherited?' she gasped out the words.

'There is no doubt of that. Of course, I realize how this must shock you . . . just as you must realize how it hurts me to talk of this. I had wanted to keep you in ignorance of the facts until it was absolutely necessary.'

'You let me fall in love first?' Mary's voice was bitter and denouncing.

'Would you rather have known first?'

Mary covered her face with her hands. No, no, she would not have wanted to know. She would not have wanted to forgo what might be the only perfect happiness in her life.

'I see by your silence that you would not. I am not altogether inhuman, Mary, or insensitive to your feelings. Perhaps I did wrong not to encourage you to take up a career of some kind . . . something to compensate for marriage.'

'Compensate?' The words were wrung from Mary's lips. What existed in the world that could compensate for Paul's love . . . for marriage to the man she loved? 'Then you're telling me I have no right to marry Paul?'

'I didn't say that. You must decide for yourself, Mary. You told me you really loved this young doctor. True love means true unselfishness . . . no personal desire should stand in the way of a loved one's happiness. If, of course, Paul does not want children then you have nothing to fear. He need never be told the truth.'

'But he does want children!' Mary cried and straight from her heart. 'He was one of six children himself and he believes in large families. Oh, Aunt

Ethel, I cannot bear it . . . *I cannot bear it*!'

The sobs broke from her throat and for a few moments the older woman was weakened in her resolve . . . weakened with treacherous thoughts that maybe she had no right to do this . . . not even for Jackie's sake. Dr. Law had assured her that in time Jackie would accept some other young girl in Mary's place. If that were so, in fact, was she doing a terrible thing to her niece.

She had always been very fond of Mary . . . and loved the little girl as her own daughter until Jackie's birth had sent the child to second place. As her son's mental unbalance became apparent, every other thought and concern had been relegated to unimportance and remained so . . . even to the exclusion of her own husband.

It was not, of course, true that she had been told Jackie's was a family disease. The big London specialists had all told her the same thing . . . that something had been injured by that fall and could never be put right, and that she must try to accept it as inevitable.

If there were anyone to blame, it was herself. The guilt lay always deep down in her heart that she, his mother, had left him in inexperienced hands. Perhaps because of this, her phobia for Jackie's well-being and comfort was the more accentuated. She had let Mary devote herself to the boy with no thought of the possible consequences and it was far too late when at last she saw her own folly.

She had tried to discourage Mary's love for Paul Deal ... but without success. Now it was in existence and in the long sleepless nights while Mary had been away from home, she had slowly come to her decision ... to prevent this marriage at all costs. 'Mary is young,' she had told herself. 'She'll get over it. I can make it up to her ... I can even start to look after Jackie more myself so Mary can get out, or get a middle-aged woman as

Nanny governess, a really reliable, experienced woman I can trust. Then, if Jackie likes her and ceases to need Mary so much, she can fall in love again and marry someone else.'

It was so long since she herself had given thought to her own marriage and how much she had loved Tom, that she could forget the desperation of love . . . the single-mindedness and enduring quality of the real emotion. Perhaps she had never really felt it. Her character was by no means as deep as Mary's and only through her unreasonable attachment to her helpless child had she ever been driven to real depths and extremes of emotion. Her affection for Tom had been true and sincere enough but she had often wondered if she could not have been just as happy with some other man, and most probably she could have been.

So she was not fully aware of the dreadful thing she was doing to her niece by placing such poisonous and untrue barriers between her and the man she wanted to marry. But she did pause for a moment, touched in spite of her iron resolve by Mary's stricken face and broken sobs. Then her will overcame her heart and she told herself again that she would see that Mary had another chance of marriage . . . could find some way when that time came to disprove the theories she had just put forward. The girl was only twenty . . . at twenty one did not know the meaning of love in its truest sense.

'You must do as you think best!' she said as kindly as she could. 'Perhaps you might have one or two normal children . . . maybe all of them would be perfectly all right. It is for you to decide whether you should take that chance.'

'I wouldn't mind . . . even if it happened. I'd love my baby as I love Jackie . . . however he was born!' Mary cried. 'But Paul . . . no, I cannot take that chance for him, Aunt Ethel.'

Mrs. Bradbourne smiled triumphantly. Then a new idea assailed her.

'Maybe *he* will be unwilling to give *you* up, Mary. He is older than you are . . . and might not be so ready to end this affair . . . at least without good reason.'

'I'll never tell him the reason . . . never!' Mary vowed, the tears falling silently down her cheeks now. 'It must be a clean break . . . a final one if it is to be borne by either of us.'

'And how can you achieve that?'

'I don't know! I'll think of something.'

Mary stood up slowly and her face was now dead-white, her eyes tear-filled and enormous with her suffering.

'I'm going to my room, Aunt Ethel. Please . . . don't say anything to Uncle Tom . . . yet!'

Alone in her bedroom, she gave way to the agony of mind in a flood of tears that eased some tiny part of her pain.

'Paul . . . Paul!' she wept. 'If I loved you less, I might deceive you . . . and we could both be happy for a while.

Will you find some other girl . . . someone who can give you perfect children . . . the children we *might* have had?'

She knew suddenly, with a mixture of pain and pride, that Paul would not give her up for this reason. He was a doctor and he must understand such things and maybe would not place such importance on them as other people. She never doubted his true love for her and knew that in his place she would not have broken their engagement. She would have agreed to anything . . . to remaining childless, to adopting children . . . or to take their chance. But even if he were prepared to make such a sacrifice for her, she could not allow him to do so. She must find some other way . . . a less painful way . . . a way which might open up some new vista for him.

She knew suddenly what she must do. She must let Paul believe that she did not after all love him enough to marry him. She could not hope to get away with such a change of behaviour in an instant, but she could in a few weeks, slowly but surely make him see she had begun to doubt herself. It would hurt terribly to do this to him, but in the end it would help him. His love would turn to hate and in a while he could find someone else . . .

His mother would understand! she thought, if she ever knew. She would thank me for doing this to Paul.

Her fingers touched the engagement ring and she bent her head and kissed the cold stones. She must take it off . . . return it to Paul . . . and with it all hope of happiness for herself. For she would never marry . . . never fall in love again. Her initiation into the sweetness of love had ended so soon . . . so very soon. If only she had dared to give herself to Paul fully and completely that night at his home.

Paul! Paul! I love you!

And all night long, she fought against the love that had so soon to be buried for evermore. And she dreaded the coming of a new day. It never once occurred to the girl, always so honest and truthful herself, to doubt what her Aunt had told her. Her confidence in human nature was trusting and absolute.

9

Tired out as she was when morning came, Mary's iron resolve to do as she had planned was unweakened. Jackie was particularly trying. Perhaps because her holiday away had left him with a feeling of insecurity, he dogged her round the house and made repeated demands on her time and attention. She tried to keep patience with him and to hide from him her own unhappiness. She had taken care to avoid her Uncle at breakfast, not coming downstairs until he had left the house. She could not have stood his concern, for he must surely see from her ravaged face that something terrible had destroyed the happiness of last evening. Nor could she bear to answer his questions. She wondered if her Aunt had said anything to him. But perhaps he did not know the truth.

Maybe her Aunt had never told him!

It was barely ten o'clock when the phone rang. In a sudden panic Mary rushed to her Aunt and told her that if it was Paul, she must say she was out . . . anything at all so that she need not speak to him.

But it appeared Paul was not going to be put off lightly. He had asked her Aunt when she would be back and he rang again at eleven and at twelve. Mary had no alternative but to answer his third call.

'Darling, you at last! I hope nothing has gone wrong? Your Aunt sounded very distant.'

His voice tore at her heart and for a moment she could not find words to answer him.

'Hullo, Paul!' she said at last.

'I've missed you terribly!' Paul's voice came to her as clearly as if he were in the room. 'Is there any chance of seeing you this evening?'

Had things been different she would have asked him to dinner . . . to

178

celebrate . . . to be welcomed by her family as his had welcomed her. But now that could not be.

'I'm terribly sorry, Paul, but . . . but Jackie isn't well. I'm afraid my going away upset him a little and I don't think I ought to come out tonight.'

There was a moment of silence and then Paul said slowly, his disappointment audible to her in his tone:

'All right, darling, if you'd rather not. What about tomorrow?'

'Yes . . . I'll try!' Mary said weakly. This was so much harder than she had imagined it would be.

'Mary . . . *is* anything wrong? Your people haven't objected to the engagement?'

'Not . . . not exactly!' Mary said with difficulty. 'My Aunt thinks . . . she thinks I'm rather young . . . that we should wait a little while before we get married.'

'Look, Mary . . . ' Paul began, and then stopped. This was what he had feared. That Aunt of hers was trying to come between them. Well, he would not stand for it. Mary was quite old enough at twenty to know her own mind . . . and to be married. Many girls much younger than Mary were married and had children at twenty. But he could not discuss it over the telephone. It could wait until he saw her tomorrow. And he would see that they did meet. He would call at the house without warning and Mrs. Bradbourne would have to show her hand if she dared. She could not deny him entry without good reason. And if it came to open warfare, then maybe that would be best in the end. Mary must choose between the past and the future. If her love were not strong enough, then he had better know it now.

'Look! darling, I have to go now. I'll see you tomorrow and we can talk then. I love you, Mary. Remember that!'

'I . . . I'll remember!' Mary said, and with a mixture of pain and thankfulness, replaced the receiver. Tears filled her eyes again, tears partly caused by fatigue and partly by the thought of all she was throwing away. How would she be brave enough to make the final break? To tell Paul that she did not love him enough . . . that she had made a mistake . . . and convince him that she spoke the truth.

Again she avoided her Uncle when he came home by retiring early to her bedroom with a headache. Aunt Ethel had tactfully suggested she might do so and she had grabbed at the straw.

'Perhaps you would like me to tell your Uncle that you are a bit upset? That you are not quite so sure of yourself or your wish to continue this engagement?'

'Thank you!' Mary said. 'You're being very kind, Aunt Ethel!'

A faint look of guilt crossed the woman's swiftly averted face. Then her mouth hardened. No, she was not being kind . . . not to Mary. But she was doing her best for her son. Jackie's behaviour today had only increased her resolutions. He had been quiet and sullen while Mary was away, the usual behaviour to precede one of his fits. Mary's return had no doubt averted that, but clearly he would not have her out of sight and his mother did not like to imagine what might have happened had Mary remained away longer.

It never occurred to Mrs. Bradbourne that the child's behaviour, far from being abnormal, was that of any normal child of five who had all his life been thoroughly spoilt. He had always had Mary and his mother at his beck and call, each trying to find new ways to amuse and entertain him, each willing to sacrifice anything in the world for his pleasure, his happiness. In his simplicity, it had not occurred to him, who lived from day to day, that things might change. And he had resented Mary not being there when he wanted her to play with him. His mother had offered to play but she was not as clever as Mary . . . she did not always let him win. His sullenness was merely an indication of his resentment.

Another long night of agony passed for Mary, to be followed by an equally anxious morning as she waited for and yet dreaded Paul's promised phone call. But the bell did not ring and she knew a sudden quite unreasonable fear that he was angry with her . . . that he was deliberately doing this to torment her!

When the front-door bell rang at half past one, they had barely finished clearing the lunch table. She had just put Jackie down for his afternoon rest when she heard from the upper landing Paul's voice in the hall below.

'May I see Mary, Mrs. Bradbourne?'

Colour flared in Mary's cheeks and her heart raced. Her knees seemed unable to support her and she clung weakly to the banister. Her Aunt's voice was inaudible to her but Paul's voice, raised and slightly angry, came clearly:

'Perhaps Mary could decide if she is well enough to see me. Would you be so good as to ask her?'

She backed through the open doorway of her bedroom where her Aunt found her.

'Well, do you wish me to send him away?'

'No!' Mary whispered. 'I'll have to see him, but don't leave me, Aunt. Stay with me whatever he says.'

'Very well!'

Watching her come down the stairs and remembering the first time he had called to fetch her to take her dancing, Paul felt his heart contract. *What had happened to her?* She looked deathly white and quite seriously ill. So her Aunt had not after all lied about Mary's health.

'Darling!' he took a step towards her but she clung to her Aunt's arm for support and seemed not to see his outstretched hand.

'Shall we go into the drawing-room?' Without waiting for a reply, Mrs. Bradbourne led the way with Mary, and with an anxious heart Paul followed them in.

Watching the older woman sit down beside Mary, Paul said almost rudely:

'Can I not see Mary alone? I'm sure she is not in need of a chaperone!'

'It's just as Mary wishes!' the woman returned smoothly. Paul swung round to look into Mary's face, but her eyes were downcast and her voice so soft that he barely heard her words as she told him she wished her Aunt to stay.

Paul shrugged his shoulders help-lessly. What *was* wrong? What had happened to the radiant girl he had left on the doorstep only a day and a half ago? Was Mary ill? Why did she want her Aunt there?

'Mary, at least grant me the privilege of seeing you alone!' he said at last. 'What is wrong? Please tell me what is going on? I don't understand.'

Mary struggled for words. This was worse than anything she had ever dreamed of. It was like some dreadful nightmare from which she *must* wake up. Paul's anxiety struck her heart like a physical blow.

'I . . . I'd rather my Aunt stayed. I . . . Paul, I'm afraid you'll be very angry with me . . . but . . . but I want to break off our engagement.'

'Angry!' the words burst from Paul's lips as he looked from Mary to her Aunt and back again. 'I just can't believe it, Mary . . . I won't believe it. What have I done to cause you to change your mind?'

'It . . . it isn't anything you have done, Paul!' the words seemed to be dragged up from deep within her. 'It's me . . . my fault. I . . . I thought I wanted to . . . to marry you. I really *did* mean it, Paul . . . ' she broke off helplessly.

'*Did* mean it?' he repeated, his heart pounding furiously. 'Then you don't any more? Tell me in simple words, Mary, don't you love me still? Why have you changed? What has changed you?'

'Paul . . . don't shout at me!' He had not realized he was shouting. 'I know it's difficult for you to understand . . . that you must hate me now . . . but

... but I was carried away ... by everything ... your family ... and it was all so ... so exciting. No one had ever proposed to me before ... and I was flattered ... and thought I had fallen in love. But when I came home ... and thought about it ... I began to realize ... the truth. Paul, I'm sorry!'

'It's something *she* has said to you!' Paul swung round and challenged Mary's Aunt openly. 'She has influenced you against me ... for God knows what reason. You have never liked me, have you? Right from the start you tried to put a spoke in our wheel. Well, have the honesty to come out into the open and tell me to my face why you object to me? Why you have turned Mary against me?'

Tears were running down Mary's cheeks. She got up and stood between Paul and her Aunt, who had made no answer to Paul's accusation.

'Paul, don't ... please. It isn't anything my Aunt said ... not directly. Naturally she ... she pointed out to me the responsibilities of marriage . . . the finality. I . . . I realized then that it wasn't just a question of having a good time and being happy together. I . . . I thought it over and knew I couldn't . . . couldn't be your wife. Paul, try to understand.'

'Understand? *I can't, Mary*. It's too sudden. And you're afraid of something. There's more to all this than a change of heart. You . . . you of all people, don't change your mind suddenly. And I will not believe you are a coward, Mary.'

'A coward?' she repeated.

'You dare not face me without your Aunt here to back you up!'

Mary looked at her Aunt helplessly. It was true! If she were to continue with this as she must, then what was to be said lay between herself and Paul only.

'Will you leave us alone?' she asked her Aunt, and as the older woman hesitated, she said: 'Please, Aunt Ethel!'

Immediately the door closed behind her, Paul went to take Mary in his arms, but she evaded him and said quickly:

'Don't, Paul, *please*! Can't you see that that is the one thing I want most to avoid. You have over-persuaded me, with words and kisses. What I feel deep down myself is something else. The me you believed in . . . believed loved you . . . was reflecting your own wishes.'

Paul's voice was hard, as he intended it to be.

'And when exactly did you realize this?'

'Yesterday, last night, the night before. Paul, please believe me . . . I've thought about this until I'm utterly exhausted by thinking. I know I'm doing the right thing. Don't make me weak . . . don't make it too hard for me.'

His eyebrows raised.

'Then you are afraid, Mary . . . afraid that I might talk you out of this sudden change of heart. You don't trust yourself very far, do you? I think I have more trust in you than you have in yourself.

It may sound conceited to say this but I believe you still love me . . . I believe you have never stopped loving me. I believe that your Aunt has frightened you with her talk of responsibilities and finality. Of course marriage holds those things . . . but they are not to be feared. There are two people to face up to the responsibilities of life instead of each one alone. And, if you wish to take a view which I don't really care for myself, there is always the divorce court. What is it you really fear, Mary? What is behind all this? You've got to tell me the truth!'

Mary was in agony. She had not thought that Paul would react like this . . . that he would quite simply refuse to accept her decision. In desperation, she took the ring off her finger and with trembling hands offered it to him. For a long moment, he looked down at her hands, and then, terrifyingly into her eyes. She dropped her lashes instantly but not before he had glimpsed the agony in them.

'I will not take it until you look me in the eyes and tell me directly that you do not love me!'

Tormented as she was, Mary felt the strength leave her legs and she stumbled backwards and all but fell into a chair. Tears coursed down her cheeks and she hid her face in her hands. She felt Paul try to pull her hands away as he knelt beside her . . . knew that in a moment, she would be weakened utterly . . . just as she always weakened to his touch.

'Don't . . . don't!' she cried. 'Why can't you leave me? Can't you understand that I don't want to marry you any more? Please go away . . . please, please!'

Slowly, Paul got to his feet. There was a look in his eyes that would have frightened Mary . . . not a look of despair . . . not a look of a beaten man, but the opposite. He was quite convinced now that Mary still loved him . . . and for the time being, that was all he required to know. He would find some way to get at the truth.

191

Clearly Mary was in no state now to continue the argument, if you could call it that, and he would not force it from her when she was so obviously ill.

'Speaking as a doctor,' he said calmly, 'I think you should go straight to bed. I'll ask Dr. Law to call round as soon as he can and bring a sedative. Good-bye, Mary!'

He walked to the door and opened it and, without moving, closed it again. As he had expected, Mary's head shot up and her arms moved instinctively in a gesture of suppliance, believing as she did that he had gone. Perhaps it was unfair of him to trick her so, yet Paul had done it because he had to be absolutely sure she did love him. Now he had no doubt and, without speaking, he opened the door again and closed it a second time, behind him.

True to his word, he sent his partner round to Mary that afternoon, having first told him the whole story.

'There is some reason her Aunt has given her that has convinced her she cannot marry me. But she loves me . . . I know that. Can't you give me any idea why this might have happened? You have known the family for years! If anyone can give me an idea, you can.'

The older man frowned.

'It doesn't make sense to me . . . not if the girl really does love you in spite of what she says.'

'She could not bring herself to say she did not, in actual words. All she really said is that she could not marry me.'

Dr. Law tapped his desk with a pencil.

'I suppose she can't be thinking that . . . that she has no right to marry you?'

'No right?' Paul questioned.

'That she thinks she might give you children like Jackie?'

'But you told me when I first went to attend the child that there had been an accident — that there was no question of an hereditary disease.'

'Perhaps the girl thinks so!'

For a moment, Paul hoped. It would explain so much. Then his face fell.

'But her Aunt must know the truth. And she was in the room most of the time. She knew of Mary's decision and obviously agreed with it. Mary must have asked the truth about her cousin years ago . . . '

'Well, I don't know. I suppose it is always possible her Aunt could have lied about it . . . but for what reason? I've known Ethel Bradbourne for years and she would never do such a terrible thing . . . I'm sure of it.'

'I'm not so sure!' Paul said quietly. 'She has never liked me . . . or certainly never approved of me as a future husband for Mary. She made no pretence about it. She might well have lied to Mary to prevent her marrying me.'

'I cannot believe any woman would do such a thing. It's terrible . . . even to contemplate. I'll admit that she is obsessed with her son's happiness . . . she told me herself that she feared the day Mary left him. But I assured her as her doctor and her friend that he would get used to doing without Mary

194

in time. No, put that idea out of your mind, Paul. There may be some other reason. I'll see if I can find out when I go round.'

But Paul could not put the idea from his mind and when Dr. Law returned from his visit he admitted his failure to obtain anything from Mary except that she no longer wished to marry him or even to see him again.

'Poor little lass was crying her heart out!' he said. 'You're quite certain you are not mistaken, my boy? Girls do change their minds, you know . . . their privilege! And she's very young.'

Paul's mouth closed tightly. He knew sincerity when he saw it and Mary had been utterly sincere when she had accepted his ring and spoken of marrying him in the spring. And she was above all honest . . . more honest than anyone he could think of. She had not even tried to hide her love when she first discovered it and might have been excused for keeping him guessing a while. She had been radiant with happiness all the time she had been at his home.

Suddenly Paul had an idea. Mary had become very friendly in those short days with his sister, Jean. Jean was a woman-of-the-world . . . might understand what was going on in Mary's mind. If he could only get them together he felt sure his young sister would get at the truth. How could he achieve it?

On impulse, he sat down and wrote in fullest detail to Jean. She was back in her London flat now, where she stayed when the M.P. for whom she worked was at Westminster.

' . . . can you find some way of meeting Mary? Maybe she would come up to stay with you in town if you invited her? Don't take no for an answer, Jean. You have always been a darned good sister to me. Don't let me down now . . . and, Jean, don't tell Mother or the family yet.

Yours in desperation,
Paul.'

Her answer came within forty-eight hours, the longest two days Paul had ever spent in his life. He devoured her letter like a starving man.

'Dearest Paul,
I have crossed the first hurdle in your noble cause! I telephoned Mary today . . . '

he glanced at the date and saw that it was yesterday's . . .

' . . . having decided against writing an invitation as it's so easy to write one's refusal in return. As I suspected, Mary was unwilling to come to the telephone but I insisted until that Aunt of hers finally fetched her when I said it was very urgent. I told Mary a whopper! that I had 'flu and no one to look after me; Mother was too busy to come up and there just wasn't anyone I knew in London who could help me out. Did she think it terribly presumptuous of me to ask my future sister-in-law to come to my aid? I think I sounded very frail but unfortunately I don't look it. Anyway, it took your Mary a long time to find an answer. At last she said she thought I ought to know that you and she were no longer engaged. I sounded sufficiently surprised and then told her I supposed she wouldn't want to come. Again a long pause (incidentally I'll expect you to pay for that call!) and then she said she would come so long as I promised not to talk about you. I rather think you're right after all, Paul, about her being afraid. I wasn't quite convinced when I got your epistle . . . after all, she could have changed her mind . . . you're not all that of a catch are you, Beautiful?

So there we are. She's coming up tomorrow and I'll have to break my promise not to talk about you and try to scrub the rude red of good health from my cheeks. Fortunately my M.P. is away this week-end and I'm free *to languish in my bed . . . rather a change for me, what?*

Don't worry, darling. I'll ring you just as soon as I've got a line for you, but don't expect anything for a day or two as I can't very well phone with Mary here, or get her to post a letter addressed to you, can I?

Ever your devoted
Sherlock Holmes.'

Paul grinned as he put the letter back in his pocket. There was a lot to be said for a large family and in particular for a grown-up sister. Jean was a bit of a worry to their Mother with her modern ways and independence but she was still the same Jean underneath . . . good, kind, trustworthy and the best friend he had ever had.

For the first time for two days, he had a good night's sleep.

10

An outsider would have seen that the patient looked a good deal better than the nurse! But it never occurred to Mary to doubt Jean's feigned illness and she set about tidying the tiny flat and making Jean as comfortable as she could.

Jean had been shocked by Mary's appearance . . . such a vast change from the glowing happy girl she had last seen at the New Year Party. Mary looked ghastly . . . deathly pale with enormous violet shadows beneath her eyes.

Now that she had come, she found herself glad to be away from home. She had not dared to leave the house for fear she might see Paul's car in the street, or that he might try to phone her or come again to see her. When he did not, her heart had bled, thinking how quickly and easily his love for her had died. He had only resisted her decision a little while . . . he could not have loved her so deeply after all. The knowledge hurt her cruelly even while her common sense told her it must be better for them both this way.

To be away from the surroundings in which she had had to break with Paul was in a way a relief, even while it was Paul's sister with whom she was staying. There was a look of Paul in Jean . . . a family likeness which caused her terrible heartache, and yet there was comfort, too, in being close to him again through Jean.

She felt an ever-increasing desire to confide in Jean . . . to have someone from Paul's family to confirm her own belief for Paul's happiness. Suppose Jean should consider that they should marry and take their chance? Suppose she thought the decision should be left to Paul? But even as she allowed this glimmer of hope, Mary rejected it as unworthy. Paul might be tempted and later regret it.

A little bitterly, she thought that Paul did not seem to be so much in love that he would fight very long or very hard for her. His silence hurt her desperately. She wondered if he had already written to tell his family of their broken engagement, of the ring her Aunt had found on the drawing-room carpet and she had sent in a registered envelope to Paul's digs.

'You know, I feel a little guilty bringing you up to town to look after me,' Jean broke in on her thoughts. It was evening and the two girls were cosily installed in the bed-sitting-room, supper cleared away and washed up by Mary in the adjoining kitchenette. 'I feel so much better I think I could get up.'

'It's horrible being ill all alone,' Mary said, 'and I am only sorry I couldn't come yesterday. My Aunt had a nasty attack of 'flu just when I first met — ' She broke off, realizing she had been about to mention Paul's name. Jean swiftly grabbed at her opportunity and filled in his name.

'I know you don't wish to talk about Paul,' she said, 'but surely you would be happier if you did, Mary. You look so tormented.'

Sudden tears sprang to Mary's eyes. Jean's quiet sympathy was almost more than she could bear.

'Mary, tell me what happened. You were so happy when I saw you last . . . and so much in love. Can't you give me some reason for breaking your engagement? I know it isn't really my business but I don't want to question Paul about something that would hurt him to talk of.'

'He . . . he doesn't know . . . the real reason!' Mary said in a whisper.

'I don't understand!' Jean encouraged her confidence. 'You've broken your engagement to Paul without telling him why? Is that fair to him?'

'Yes! No! Oh, Jean . . . I can't tell him. I wanted him to believe I had stopped loving him . . . as if I ever can! I hoped that he would forget me after a while and find some other girl who . . . who could give him everything he deserves.'

'What is it that you can't give him, Mary?' Jean asked quietly. 'All of us at home who know Paul so well believe that you can give him everything in the world he needs from the woman he loves. For he does love you, Mary. You don't doubt that, do you?'

'I don't know . . . but that is not why I broke our engagement, Jean. I believed at the time that he did love me. Perhaps he still does.'

'Then why, Mary, *why?*'

Jean held her breath, knowing that at last she was to hear the truth that had been denied Paul for some mysterious reason at which she could not guess.

'Because I cannot give him children!' The words came in a flat monotone.

'You mean you are unable to conceive a child?'

'No! But . . . Jean, my little cousin is not . . . not normal. He has something lacking in his brain. I learned when I came back from my visit to you that my children . . . Paul's children, might be the same. I had always believed Jackie's troubles to have begun after his nurse fell downstairs with him as a baby. Jean, I love Paul too much to cause him the unhappiness and distress my Aunt and Uncle must have felt . . . or ever to cause him to regret marrying me.'

Jean stared at the younger girl in dismay.

'But, Mary, how could you not have known of this years ago? Didn't your Aunt tell you?'

Mary shook her head.

'She didn't think it necessary until I was old enough to marry . . . and you see, Paul and I fell in love so unexpectedly. I'd never given a thought to the future myself because I had never been in love before and the fact that I might one day marry seemed so remote.'

Jean searched her mind for the wording of Paul's long letter. She recalled with sudden excitement the paragraph that had told her of Dr. Law's statement that it could have nothing to do with Jackie since the child's disease was not hereditary. *Why should Mary believe that it was?* Surely her Aunt would not have told her such a terrible lie?

'How do you know you and Paul would have children like your cousin?' she asked carefully.

'We might not have, but we could. My Aunt explained this to me when I told her Paul and I were engaged. She said that if I truly loved Paul and wanted his happiness, I could never marry him. Because I agreed with her, I had no alternative but to give Paul back his ring.'

'But you should have given him the real reason,' Jean said thoughtfully. 'He is a doctor, Mary, and he would have understood and appreciated the medical aspect of the whole thing. Surely you don't imagine he hasn't already considered it? He had met your little cousin before he asked you to marry him?'

'Yes!' Mary nodded. 'But even Dr. Law doesn't know the truth. We moved to a new house about six months after the accident and my Aunt let everyone believe that was the cause. Oh, Jean, what does it all matter now? It's over, finished, and Paul has gone out of my life. I think he was in the end quite glad to go. You see, I must have hurt his pride when I told him I had stopped loving him.'

'And you think he believed it? Mary, you of all people are incapable of deceit. I don't believe you convinced Paul.'

'Yet he has made no effort to see me again.'

She recounted the details of that terrible afternoon when Paul had bade her good-bye.

Jean was torn by indecision. Mary's revelation of her true reasons for throwing Paul over were so far from what she had imagined ... or Paul, who had told her Dr. Law stated without doubt that Jackie's brain had been injured in the accident. Now what would Paul wish her to do? Reveal the truth . . . if it was the truth. Could Paul's elderly partner have been wrong? Did Mary's Aunt know something of which Paul and Dr. Law were ignorant? And if it were after all so, would Paul let that stand in the way of his marriage to Mary?

'Tell me exactly what your Aunt told you!' she asked Mary. The younger girl was glad to do so. Painful as it was for her to speak it was still a relief to unburden her thoughts.

Jean's face hardened. Paul had not omitted in his letter his suspicions of Mary's Aunt . . . his belief that she would stoop to anything if she believed it to be for her child's good. It seemed fantastic that any woman could do such a thing . . . and to the girl who had lived under her roof and done so much for the little boy. But Paul believed her to be obsessed with her child.

' . . . she is at a difficult time of life,'
Paul had written . . . 'and emotional
women can do queer things for
which they cannot be held entirely
responsible. But you probably know
about it so I won't go into medical
details. I think I should want to
commit murder if this turned out to
be so, even while as a doctor I can
see that she might be momentarily
unbalanced at the thought of losing
Mary who has always been such a
devoted nurse and companion to the
boy . . . '

Now Jean had little doubt as to the
truth of the whole matter. She prayed
silently and fervently that Mary would
not try to extract a promise from her
not to repeat this conversation to Paul.
Fortunately Mary seemed so resigned
to the inevitability and hopelessness of
the whole affair that she had not
considered Paul might be making these
enquiries through her, Jean.
In a way, it was wrong to betray a

confidence, but Jean had no hesitation in doing so in this case. As soon as she decently could, she would get word to Paul and then it would be up to him to act as he thought best. Both his and Mary's happiness was at stake . . . depending on a word from her.

Jean appeared to have made such a miraculous recovery next day that Mary decided she could go home. She was not sure she wanted to . . . to face her Uncle's silent sympathy or her Aunt's cold approval. But Jean did not press her to stay although she warmly invited her to come up again soon on a purely social visit.

'We'll do a flick together and have some supper out . . . just the two of us!' Jean said, for she knew that Mary would not be interested in any escort she might provide.

Mary had been gone only a few minutes when Jean grabbed the telephone and gave Paul's number. Dr. Law's nurse answered her and told her that both men were out although Dr. Deal was expected back for surgery at six o'clock.

'Can't you tell me where I can get hold of him now?' Jean asked impatiently. 'It's very urgent.'

'Well, I think he was going over to the hospital,' the nurse informed her. 'You might try there.'

Jean tried and failed, and it was not until a quarter to six that she finally reached Paul, at his digs.

'You only just caught me. I'm due at the surgery at six!' he told her. 'I presume Mary is not there?'

'She went home this afternoon,' Jean told him excitedly. 'Paul, I've found out everything you want to know.'

As quickly as she could, she recited the gist of their conversation. 'Her Aunt gave Mary to believe that the London specialists had told her the accident was not responsible for Jackie's condition, and that Dr. Law was wrong when he informed you it was not hereditary. The Aunt says it is.'

Paul tried to calm his many conflicting emotions.

'That is quite ridiculous. Dr. Law would have gone most fully into the boy's case history when they came to the district. He would know of any specialist consultation he may have had. Jean, you're a darling . . . I could hug you, and I could murder that woman. To think she might have got away with it . . . it's a dastardly thing to do.'

'Then you're certain she has lied?'

'Absolutely, and I'll prove it. But even if she hasn't, do you think I'd care? Well, of course I'd care, as much for Mary's sake as my own, but it wouldn't stop me marrying her. I love her, Jean. I don't think I even realized myself how much until I looked like losing her.'

'Well, let me know how things transpire!' Jean said. 'Now you've embroiled me in this I'm almost as tensed up as you are.'

'If I can, I'll get Mary out of that house!' Paul said violently. 'She can go to Mother . . . or to you, if you'll have her. I won't let her stay there any longer!'

'Paul, steady on, old fellow!' Jean cautioned him. 'You forget that they are her relations . . . almost mother and father to her.'

'Do you think she will have much love for her Aunt when she finds out what she so nearly contrived to do?'

'Perhaps not, but her Uncle may not have been in on it, and besides, Paul, she loves the child. Don't try to separate her from those she loves or she might really turn against you.'

Paul bit his lip. There was something in what his sister said. Mary did love Jackie . . . and this was a force he would have to contend with. Although every instinct in him demanded that she should be removed as quickly as possible from her Aunt's influence, reason told him that it might not be Mary's wish. And in any event, Mary would not be likely to trust her Aunt again.

His next job was to find proof . . . proof for Mary. He did not care about himself.

He said good-bye to Jean, and climbed into his car with a singing heart. She still loved him . . . and he would win her after all.

11

With Dr. Law's help, and with the aid of some old records, proof was easily come by. Paul actually held in his hand a letter from the greatest of all brain specialists, giving his opinion clearly and without room for argument.

'What next?' he asked Dr. Law, who had been considerably shaken at what Paul had revealed.

'I don't know, Paul. Ethel will have to be shown this letter, of course. I still find it hard to believe that she knew the truth. She must have been under some misapprehension. Maybe she misunderstood the specialist.'

'I don't think so!' Paul said, his voice hard. 'But I am quite willing, if you think it best, that Mary should be allowed to think so. I don't want her hurt any more than I can help. But Mrs. Bradbourne shall know that I know the truth. I intend Mary to be my wife and I cannot risk the same kind of thing happening a second time.'

'I can understand your bitterness, Paul, but you have at least offered to do the magnanimous thing as regards Mary. I think you are right. Cannot you extend the benefit of the doubt to Mrs. Bradbourne?'

'No, I cannot!' Paul said. 'I dare not would be more true to say. When I first suspected the truth from what Jean told me, I wanted to extract revenge at any cost. But I've thought about it since then and calmed down a little. I don't want to be revenged now . . . that would be childish. Above all, I don't want Mary hurt, but can't you see that if we let that woman think she has got away with it this time, she may try something else? If she will go to such lengths once, she could do so again. Unless I am to take Mary right away from her family and the child, I lay her and myself open to any similar scheme.'

Dr. Law looked at his young partner and sighed.

'Once Mary is your wife, Paul, Ethel would have no reason for trying to keep you apart. Mary would already have left home and Ethel will presumably have to find someone to take Mary's place unless she intends to look after the boy herself. As her doctor I don't advise that. She is going through a bad spell and I don't think she's good for him in her emotional state. I shall recommend her to get a nurse. Be compassionate, Paul, if you can. She will hate you all your life if you let her see you doubt her motive. In her heart she will probably guess the truth. Let her save her face if you can!'

Paul drew a deep breath. There was something in what Dr. Law said. What harm could Mrs. Bradbourne do once he and Mary were married? He would have this knowledge to hold over her head should things go wrong a second time. At present he could well afford to hold back his hand. He had liked Mary's Uncle very much and even thought how pleasant it would be to have them to their home now and again and to visit them. Now he could never bring himself to like Mary's Aunt but they could perhaps learn to be civil to one another . . . for Mary's sake.

'How do you advise me to go about this?' he asked the older man, whose opinion he respected.

'Would you prefer that I spoke to Mrs. Bradbourne? I've been a friend of the family for so many years. I'll talk to her, and afterwards to Mary, telling her her Aunt made a mistake. Then you can see Mary and put on that ring again, eh?'

Paul nodded.

'You'll go tonight?'

'Very well!' Dr. Law said. 'You'd better answer any calls for me while I'm gone, Paul.'

★   ★   ★

It seemed hours to Paul before Dr. Law returned, although in fact he had been gone only an hour. He looked tired but he greeted Paul with a smile.

'After all, you were right,' he told the young man. 'Ethel Bradbourne went to pieces when I showed her the letter . . . more or less admitted that she had done this because she had been so worried about her son. She begged me not to tell her husband . . . he knew nothing at all about it and had been told by her not to question Mary or press her for any reason since it would distress her. The poor woman said he would hate her if he knew the truth, because he loves Mary almost as much as he loves his own child. So I gave my word. I saw Mary afterwards . . . let her read the letter. Poor child . . . she was so overcome, she nearly fainted. I told her you would explain everything else to her and she insisted that she see you right away.'

'You mean I'm to go over there now?' Paul asked, jumping to his feet.

Dr. Law smiled.

'I mean she is in the car, out there,' He pointed a hand vaguely at the window.

Paul was gone in a flash, and the older man sat down wearily in a chair. He had been shaken very badly by this revelation of human weakness. Suddenly he felt the futility of spending a life working to cure men's bodily ills when they could become so ill mentally. For it was a kind of mental aberration. Ethel Bradbourne was not a hard, cruel or evil woman. She had led a good life and always been kind to her niece. Yet some inner compulsion had driven her to the point where she had tried to destroy two people's happiness in order to safeguard that of her child.

A great pity for her overcame his other emotions, and he felt that Paul would be doing the right thing in refraining from confronting her with her shame.

Paul had no thought for anyone but

Mary as he ran out into the darkness. He flung open the door of the car and a moment later Mary was in his arms . . . or as nearly in his arms as the gear levers would permit! He cared nothing for what any passer-by or onlooker might think of their respectable local doctor, kissing his girl in a broad main street. Let them think as they pleased . . . Mary would soon be his wife.

Mary was crying softly . . . crying for happiness. She did not know how this wonderful thing had happened, but it did not matter. Nothing mattered now but that she was free to marry Paul . . . that he loved her and wanted her and had found some way to prove conclusively his own love. Dr. Law had said that Paul had been the one to discover the truth. So, when she had believed him to have accepted her change of heart, he had been working to discover the reason, and in doing so had discovered facts that proved her Aunt to have been entirely mistaken.

'Poor Aunt Ethel! She must be

feeling so awful at having made so terrible a mistake!'

Then the touch of Paul's lips put all other thought from her mind.

12

It had not surprised Paul when Mary had said to him: 'Of course my Aunt would never deliberately lie to me. She must have been in so distraught a state of mind that she misunderstood what the specialist said. She believed what she told me to be the truth — she must have done!'

Paul, who only a short while before had wanted his revenge at all costs, was now talking in Mrs. Bradbourne's defence. He was so wildly happy to know that all was at last finally settled between himself and Mary . . . that she had loved him enough to sacrifice her own happiness for what she had imagined ultimately to be his.

Darling, unselfish Mary! Even had Mrs. Bradbourne's dreadful lie been true, it could have made no difference to his love for her, his desire to make her his wife. Did Mary think he placed a higher value on his unborn children than on the woman he loved?

As he had poured out his thoughts to her, Mary had known the fullest possible content. But uneasiness still lay in her heart, for how could her Aunt have made a mistake in so vital a matter. She felt she could not return to the house and be forced to talk to her, to carry on as if she suspected nothing when this terrible suspicion lay between them.

'It is for so short a while, my darling!' Paul said. 'We'll be married early in March. I want time to find a house for us to live in and that might not be very easy. Try not to think about it any more. There is your Uncle to consider. He knew nothing of all this and he would be dreadfully distressed. Your Aunt begged Dr. Law not to tell her husband of her mistake, and he promised he would not. If you refuse to speak to her, then he will want a reason and will sooner or later discover everything. Your Aunt is completely broken . . . Dr. Law told me the poor woman's shame was quite awful to see.'

'It would be so dreadful if she had done it deliberately in order to separate us; if she had a reason, I have a right to know of it!' Mary cried. 'She owes me the truth . . . all of it, Paul. We cannot live together with this between us.'

Paul said thoughtfully:

'If you really do not wish to go home, darling, you can always stay with my family in Devon. They would love to have you and I shall be happy to think of you being with them, even while it would mean we would not see much if anything of one another.'

Mary's eyes brightened and then she shook her head.

'There is something even I had forgotten for the moment, Paul . . . someone very *very* dear to me . . . Jackie. I can't just walk out of *his* life. None of this was his fault, poor little boy. I shall have to stay, Paul . . . find some way of making my peace with my

Aunt . . . for Jackie's sake.'

Now she was home again, Paul's ring on her finger and his last kiss still warm upon her lips. The shock that had engulfed her when she had first begun to suspect her Aunt's duplicity was wearing off and Mary's naturally warm generous nature had reasserted itself. She felt no tiredness, although it was very late. She passed Jackie's room and paused for a moment to look in and make sure he was sleeping peacefully. Then turning her head, she noticed that a light shone from beneath her own bedroom door. Who could be in her room at this hour? A burglar? For a moment, Mary's heart-beat quickened in fright, then intuition gave her the answer. Her Aunt was there, waiting to see her.

When she at last brought herself to open the door Mary was deeply shocked by the face of the stricken woman. Tears had ravaged her face and she looked nearer sixty than forty. She was sitting on the bed, her hands folded hopelessly in her lap.

Impulsively, Mary took a step towards her, then stopped still. So it was after all true. Her Aunt had lied to her to stop her marrying Paul!

'You wanted to see me, Aunt Ethel?'

The tear-filled, red-rimmed eyes looked up to hers.

'Yes! I know what you must be thinking of me . . . how much you must hate me, Mary. I . . . I hate myself. I realize now how very wrong it was of me.'

'It was a cruel thing to do . . . and without reason!' Mary cried bitterly. 'You had nothing against Paul . . . had you?'

The older woman shook her head.

'Then why? That's what I don't understand. I had told you so often that I would never leave Jackie . . . it can't have been that.'

'But it was, *it was*! Don't you see, Mary, that your promises had been made *before* you fell in love. I knew how powerful an emotion love could be

. . . and saw with my own eyes how it changed you towards Jackie.'

'It did not!' Mary cried hotly. 'You cannot say that. My love for Paul is something quite apart from my love for Jackie.'

'Oh, yes, Mary! The emotions are different . . . but the demands on your time . . . that was something else. You gave Jackie no thought when Paul asked you down to his home . . . and at Christmas, too.'

'That is not true!' Mary cried again, anger hardening her voice. 'Paul asked me down for Christmas but I refused to go . . . because of Jackie. I went for two days at the New Year. Do you imagine I wouldn't have liked to stay longer? Nor would I have gone at all if Jackie had been ill.'

'If I could have believed that . . . '

Mary's anger left her abruptly, and with sudden calm she sat down on her bed beside her Aunt.

'You did not have much faith in me, did you, Aunt Ethel? I am beginning to understand a little. You acted as you did for Jackie . . . without malice against me.'

'I swear that's the truth!' her Aunt cried. 'I never wanted to hurt you, Mary. I thought you were young enough to get over Paul. I meant to try to accustom Jackie to someone else . . . myself, or a nursery nurse or governess, and then in a few years' time you would have been able to marry without it hurting Jackie. I would have told you then that I had made a mistake . . . even confessed that I lied . . . nothing would have mattered then. Can't you see the position I was in?'

'I can see that you never really understood how deeply Paul and I are in love; that you had no trust in me; no belief in MY love for Jackie. You must have known I would never do anything to hurt him.'

'Yet you told me you wanted to be married in the spring.'

'That Paul wanted me to marry him in the spring,' Mary corrected. 'But had you been less cold and distant with me, Aunt . . . preventing any of my confidences, I would have told you that I was willing to postpone my marriage for as long as necessary, even if it meant years. That is still true. But as I mean to marry Paul as soon as possible now it means that Jackie must start to learn to do without me . . . right away. Aunt Ethel, even when I'm married, I can continue to take him out for his afternoon walks, come to tea, have him to my home. Paul is very understanding and he knows how I love Jackie. He would not come between us. Even now, when you might imagine he would ask me never to come back to this house, he remembered Jackie . . . Paul did.'

Her Aunt covered her face with her hands and the tears began to course down her cheeks anew.

'I'm so ashamed!' she whispered.

Her humiliation was so complete that the last of Mary's defences went. She put her arms round the older woman, feeling herself now to be the elder, her Aunt the child.

'I didn't realize . . . I thought only of Jackie. He does love you so, Mary. And he's so helpless, so pathetic. I can never forget that it was my fault he had that terrible accident.'

'How can you say that, Aunt Ethel? How can you?'

'I should have looked after him myself, not entrusted him to a young nurse. I would have been more careful.'

'Aunt, you *cannot* blame yourself. Hundreds of people have nurses and nannies. Why, it is more my fault than yours. If you had not had me to look after as well, you might never have felt the need of that nurse.'

'No! I was selfish . . . I didn't want to be tied to a very young baby. You had nothing to do with it.'

'Aunt, you must not blame yourself. It was an accident . . . the purest accident. Anyone, you yourself, might have stumbled on those stairs. Have you lived all these years blaming yourself?'

Pity for her Aunt overwhelmed any other emotion.

'Then don't . . . ever again. And, Aunt, dear Aunt, never again doubt my love for Jackie. It is as deep-rooted as yours. I ought to tell you now that I'm going to marry Paul . . . soon . . . as soon as we've found a house. Paul wants it that way and I think after . . . after this, I owe it to him to fall in with his wishes. But tomorrow we'll start looking for a nice girl . . . she can share my bedroom . . . we can easily fit a divan in that corner. Then I'll spend every moment of my day showing her how we manage, the things Jackie likes to do and his routine. Eight weeks is quite a long time . . . and if Jackie is not reasonably settled with her, then I'll postpone my wedding until he is.'

'Oh, Mary!' was all her Aunt could say as the tears began again.

Practical now, Mary went downstairs and made a cup of tea. The hot drink warmed and calmed her Aunt and having given her promise to say nothing at all to her Uncle and to give him some vague idea of a quarrel with Paul now put right, Mary at last got her Aunt to bed.

But her last thoughts were of Paul ... of the deep glow of happiness and utter content she had experienced when at last they were reunited. Perhaps their love had gone all the deeper for their temporary separation. It had made each of them realize how really and truly they did love one another ... how hopeless life seemed apart.

'Darling Paul!' she whispered, and fell into the first deep sound sleep she had had for days.

★ ★ ★

The following few days were the happiest Mary could remember. Her Uncle had been delighted to learn that Mary and Paul had patched up their 'quarrel'.

'Thought it was just a lovers' tiff!' he had told her at breakfast the next

233

morning. 'Obvious to me the fellow adores you. And you love him!' He pinched her cheek and looked into the sparkling eyes. 'I'm glad, Mary dear. And your Aunt tells me she is delighted. I thought at one time she didn't approve of your young man. Can't think why. But she's changed her mind . . . the way women will. Now what about inviting Paul to dinner here tonight? Your Aunt has another of her headaches so she won't be down, but she thought it a good idea for Paul to come and have a chat with me after dinner.'

Mary had left him alone with Paul for an hour while she went upstairs to talk to her Aunt. When they called her downstairs, both men seemed very happy. Paul told her of her Uncle's very generous offer to buy a house for them as a wedding present.

'All we have to do now is to find one!' Paul said.

'There's bound to be something somewhere!' Mary cried as she hugged her Uncle. 'We'll get the house agents to send details and I'll go and look at the 'possibles' in the afternoon when I take Jackie for his walk. He'll enjoy the change, I expect.'

The days seemed to pass on swift feet. Each post brought stencilled lists of houses available in the district, and at the same time, the occasional letter in answer to their advertisement for a nurse or governess for Jackie.

Mary discussed the houses with Paul in the evenings, and the letters with her Aunt in the daytime. Over the house, they were immensely lucky. The third one Mary went to see she fell completely in love with. It was not very large but modern and labour-saving and it had huge attics which might eventually be converted into extra bedrooms if they had their large family after all! Paul came to look over it with her at the week-end and liked it as much as she did. Then Uncle Tom took over and started negotiations with the estate egents while they held their thumbs and prayed and discussed in turn how they would furnish each room when it was theirs!

But it had not proved so easy to find a young girl for Jackie. They seemed either too young . . . and her Aunt was naturally prejudiced after Jackie's accident with the young girl who had fallen downstairs . . . or they were in their late twenties and engaged to be married, wishing for a temporary job only. At last Mary and her Aunt came to the conclusion that an older woman might be easier to find and far more responsible a person to look after Jackie.

'Someone in their late thirties, early forties!' her Aunt said thoughtfully. 'Someone who has no intention of marrying but who is young enough to amuse and play with Jackie . . . '

Once they had decided on this course of action, everything went smoothly for them. A very nice woman, who gave her age as thirty-five, came to be interviewed. It transpired that she had been married and widowed during the war. Her husband had been a pilot and they had had no children. She told them she would never marry again and that she wanted a position which she could be reasonably sure would be permanent.

'I love children!' Mrs. Mayhew told them. 'I understand your little boy is backward, but I have had a V.A.D.'s training in the war and can do simple nursing if it is required.'

Mrs. Bradbourne looked from Mary to the pleasant well-educated woman and her hopes were raised.

'I expect you would like to see Jackie!' she said. Mary went with them to the nursery where Jackie looked up, gave them only a quick glance, and resumed his play.

Mrs. Mayhew knelt down and without speaking to the boy, backed one of his cars into the garage.

'Doesn't go there!' Jackie said scornfully.

'It wanted some petrol!' Mrs. Mayhew said calmly. 'And a pint of oil, please!'

Jackie's face broke into a grin.

'You're too old to play cars!' he said cheekily. Mrs. Mayhew laughed.

'All right, if you don't want me to play . . . '

Jackie gave her a doubtful look and then grinned again.

'You can play if you want,' he said. 'But they're *my* cars.'

'He doesn't usually take so well to strangers!' Mary said as they went downstairs again. 'You've found the right way with Jackie, Mrs. Mayhew.'

Terms were discussed and Mrs. Mayhew agreed to come for a month on trial. At the end of that period, both parties would know if they wished it to be made a permanent arrangement.

Mary grew to like Mrs. Mayhew even more in the ensuing week. She did not force herself on Jackie, but was always there when he wanted something and motioned Mary to remain seated while she went for it.

'He must learn to depend on me, now,' she said. And later, she confided in Mary that in her view, Jackie was not so backward as he liked to make out.

'I think he could make much more progress if he went to a school!' she said. 'A special school, of course. But maybe your Aunt does not like the idea?'

'I don't know!' Mary said doubtfully. 'You see, the doctors have always told us that he was incurable.'

'Well, doctors can be wrong. Besides, the companionship would do him good. Maybe in time I could talk to your Aunt about it.'

Mary was glad for the tact of that 'in time'. She knew her Aunt would not easily let Jackie out of her sight or let him attempt anything that might be a strain for him or make him unhappy.

Meanwhile, she was herself freer to shop for the house and her trousseau. She spent a day in London and lunched with Jean at her flat. Jean was friendly and sweet and they laughed together over her confession about the imaginary 'flu.

'You've forgiven me, Mary?' she asked her future sister-in-law.

'Forgiven!' Mary cried. 'Why, if it hadn't been for you, Paul and I might not be getting married.'

The two girls had great fun shopping and Mary found Jean's natural flair for clothes a great help in her choice. Her Aunt had been more than generous in allowing her a big cheque for her trousseau, and slowly she began to cross off the items on her carefully drawn-up list.

Long letters passed between Mary and Paul's mother, for she was to have a white wedding from her Aunt's house and Joan and Jonathon were to be bridesmaid and page, Margaret and Jean maids of honour. There were the dresses to plan and Mrs. Deal was having them made locally to Mary's design and colour scheme. Just before the big day came, the entire Deal family were coming to stay in London for two nights so that there would be time for a rehearsal.

Paul came to the house most evenings when he was not working. Sometimes the telephone would ring and he would be called away and Mary said laughing that it was good training for her for the future. They spent long hours planning the house which Uncle Tom had now bought for them, and every spare moment they could choosing furniture and furnishings.

The month of Mrs. Mayhew's trial expired and she was definitely engaged by Mrs. Bradbourne, who had promised to re-do Mary's bedroom for her after Mary had left. The divan would be pushed back against one wall, a pretty cover made with curtains to match, a wireless installed and a comfortable chair. They would also replace the little desk Mary was taking with her to her new home, and the bed-sitting-room would be complete. Mrs. Mayhew seemed delighted and spent quite a time choosing a colour scheme which her new employer had left to her to decide.

The wedding day was at last fixed for the twenty-fifth of March. Paul was to have a fortnight's leave for his honeymoon and Dr. Law had already written to obtain an assistant during that time as it was usually a busy month. He teased Paul by reminding him that he would get a nice income-tax rebate since he was marrying before the end of the financial year!

Life was at its most perfect for them all when tragedy suddenly struck at their door. It was a bright sunny day . . . with promise of spring not far away, when Mrs. Bradbourne went out after breakfast to call on the baker who was going to make the wedding cake. She had told Mary she would be back in half an hour, but an hour passed and still she did not come. Thinking she might have found some shopping to do on her way home, Mary and Mrs. King were not worried, and even when Paul's car drew up outside, Mary knew only a pleasant surprise that he should have found time to call and see her so early.

But Paul's face, as she opened the door to him, struck at her heart. His eyes were full of pity and Mary knew then that something ghastly had happened.

'Paul, what is it?'

'Come into the drawing-room, Mary, and I'll tell you. I'm afraid it is your Aunt. There was a road accident and she was very badly injured. Dr. Law was called by a passer-by . . . the surgery was only a few yards away, you see. He had no idea who it was until he got there. He went with your Aunt to the hospital . . . but . . . darling, try to bear up. I'm afraid they couldn't do anything. When the ambulance arrived, she was dead.'

13

Mary stared at Paul, her face a deathly white.

'Aunt Ethel . . . dead!'

Paul put his arms round her and forced her into a chair.

'Steady now, darling. I know this must be a terrible shock. Try to be brave about it.'

Mary seemed suddenly to be numbed to all feeling. Only her mind worked now . . . all other emotion was drained from her by the suddenness and unexpectedness of her Aunt's death.

'Uncle Tom . . . Paul, does he know?'

'Yes, darling! Dr. Law telephoned his office asking him to go to the hospital. When your Uncle arrived, it was too late for him to see her alive.'

'Poor Uncle Tom . . . poor Uncle Tom!' Mary said over and over again.

Paul, with an anxious look at her white face, left the room and found his way to the kitchen where Mrs. Mayhew was making Jackie his morning Ovaltine. He quickly told her the news and asked her if she'd mind bringing some strong sweet tea to Mary as soon as possible.

As he had expected, Mary was in tears when he returned, the full realization having at last found its way through to her heart. She was sobbing quietly and clung to Paul when he took her in his arms.

'I said such awful things about her, Paul . . . after . . . Oh, I'm glad I forgave her . . . poor darling Aunt Ethel.'

She seemed to calm down after drinking a little of the tea and at her request Paul gave her what details he knew of the accident. A lorry, swerving to avoid a small child who had run into the road, mounted the pavement. Two women who were walking towards him saw the danger in time, but Mrs. Bradbourne had her back turned and she was hit without realizing anything about it.

'She can never have felt any pain!' Paul reassured Mary. 'She was unconscious when the first passer-by reached her, and she never regained consciousness. It was a merciful death, darling, if death was to come to her in some form or another.'

'But, Paul . . . she was so young . . . and . . . she was so happy about everything now Mrs. Mayhew had settled down. She was looking forward to the wedding . . . she had a new dress . . .'

The tears came again and Paul comforted her by the silent sympathy and reassurance of his love and his presence when she most needed him.

The thought had flashed across his mind that now the wedding . . . only two weeks distant, would have to be postponed. He felt a moment of human weakness when he thought: 'Even in death she has managed to keep us apart a little longer!' But he rejected that thought as unworthy and unfair. For Mrs. Bradbourne had done everything in her power to be polite and welcoming to Paul these last months. He knew that he could never bring himself to like her although on the surface he, too, was polite and friendly. But he would never fully trust her again . . . and now, poor woman, she was dead.

Suddenly Mary sat up straight and gripped his arm.

'Paul . . . Jackie. He'll have to be told . . . how . . . how terrible!'

Paul frowned. Momentarily, his concern only for Mary, he had entirely forgotten the boy. Well, he would have to learn sooner or later that he would not see his mother again. But at least he would not fully comprehend what had happened to her.

'I think it would be best just to tell him his mother has gone away to have a long holiday and rest.' Paul suggested. 'I've no doubt he will accept that if you tell him calmly. When he asks if she is coming back, you could hint that she might not ever come and break it gradually to him that she has gone away for good. Try not to show your own unhappiness, darling. He will take his cue from you, you know.'

Paul could not have found a better way to bring Mary back to full control of herself. She squared her shoulders and took a deep breath.

'I'll never let him be unhappy about this, Paul. Aunt could never rest in peace if she thought he was fretting. I vowed I would never leave him while he needed me and I renew that now with my whole heart. Paul, darling, you do understand?'

Paul steadied himself and bit his lip.

'Mary, what are you trying to tell me?'

'Only that I must consider Jackie before myself, Paul. Surely *you* understand that. I cannot go off now and leave him alone with Mrs. Mayhew.'

'But she seems such a competent woman . . . and you told me Jackie liked her. Mary, you promised me you would never let anything come between us again. You aren't going to do that, are you?'

Mary took Paul's hand, stretched pleading towards her.

'Oh, darling, no, of course not! I couldn't do that to myself let alone to you. How could you imagine such a thing! I only meant we might have to wait a little longer to be married.'

'We must wait anyway, now,' Paul said slowly. 'Out of respect to your Aunt.'

'We won't postpone it any longer than we must. I shall have to think what to do about Jackie. I can't leave him here alone with Mrs. Mayhew.'

Paul frowned thoughtfully.

'Surely that is what you must do, Mary? Unless . . . ' he paused, fully aware of the possible implications of his unvoiced suggestion and yet the very nature of his love for Mary forcing him to make it . . . 'Unless, darling, you'd like to have him live with us?'

'Oh, Paul!' Mary cried, her eyes shining. 'Would you really let me have him?'

He was so shaken by the great light of love and gratitude that radiated from her that he quelled any inner doubts he might have had and said:

'If it is what you want, Mary. I'm fond of the boy, although I do think he's been rather spoilt. And I do think Mrs. Mayhew is right when she says he might attend one of these schools for backward children. He needs companionship.'

'But, Paul, they're *boarding* schools, aren't they?'

'Yes! But he could come home for the holidays.'

Mary shook her head.

'I couldn't let him go . . . not yet!' she said. 'Aunt Ethel was terribly against the idea and it would seem to be taking advantage of . . . of her death, to send him away now.'

Paul, seeing her distress, said quickly: 'Well, there's plenty of time to talk about it later, darling. Don't worry about it now. Don't worry about anything. Your Uncle and I will see to the necessary arrangements, and I'll see the Vicar to cancel our wedding, and let the family know.'

'Oh, Paul!'

For the first time, Mary realized that all her wonderful hopes and plans would have to be broken. There could be no wedding the week after next, no honeymoon, no lovely bridal dress to wear . . . no one to live in the new house so lovingly prepared and ready waiting for them.

She struggled against her tears of disappointment, deeming them to be selfish when at such a time she should be thinking only of Uncle Tom and poor Aunt Ethel.

'I'll have to go now, Mary!' Paul said at last. 'But tell your Uncle I'll call round after evening surgery to see if there is any way I can help. I . . . I expect they will bring your Aunt back here some time this afternoon. I suggest that you send Mrs. Mayhew out somewhere with Jackie. I'm sorry I can't stay with you, darling, but I'll be back tonight.'

During the next week, only the tremendous number of things there were for Mary to do, kept her from breaking down completely. It had taken enormous self-control to break the news in the way Paul had suggested to Jackie. Afterwards, she had hurried out to buy armfuls of flowers for the spare room which she prepared lovingly to receive her Aunt when she was brought back from the hospital.

Uncle Tom had come with his wife and Mary had been aghast to see how shock and sorrow had aged him. He looked suddenly a very old man. Paul proved himself a tower of strength. He made the arrangements for the funeral, which was an unpretentious affair though all the family friends turned up, and to Mary's surprise and pleasure, Paul's sister Jean arrived to represent her family.

At the same time, she had to cancel various arrangements she had made for her new home . . . the removal van which was to call to collect her desk and luggage and other small items of furniture her Aunt and Uncle had given her for her new home. The days seemed filled with endless little details, her evenings trying to cheer and comfort her Uncle.

At the end of that first week, he seemed to make the effort to rally himself and he called Mary into the drawing-room one evening before dinner to discuss with her what plans they must make for the future.

'I don't know what is best to do for Jackie,' he told her. 'I suppose Mrs. Mayhew would stay on here to look after him. Have you mentioned any such suggestion to her?'

'You need not worry about Jackie, Uncle Tom. Paul has said he might come to live with us when we're married. That is if you agree to the idea.'

Her Uncle gave her a sharp glance.

'I think that is wonderfully generous of Paul, but I don't know if it is such a good plan, Mary, to saddle yourself with someone else's child . . . handicapped at that . . . at the start of your marriage. You know, marriage isn't always as easy or as happy at the beginning as young lovers imagine. There are tiffs and upsets and a lot of adjusting to be done by both parties. It isn't the time to be worrying about a third party.'

'But, Uncle, Paul and I never have rows . . . and we are perfectly suited in every way!' Mary cried. 'And it was Paul who offered . . . I did not suggest it first. He knows how I love Jackie . . . how much Aunt Ethel depended on me. If she could have spoken her dying wish I know she would have put him in my care. I cannot let her down now.'

'You have your life to lead, Mary. It is not right that you should accept another's responsibilities. Your first duty when you marry is to Paul.'

'I know that, Uncle. But you don't know how wonderfully understanding and unselfish Paul is.'

Her Uncle forbore to disillusion her. He had seen so much of other couple's married differences . . . oh, it started well enough with honeymoons and all the thrill and excitement of being newly-weds. But marriage wasn't easy . . . for anyone. It meant giving as well as taking and it nearly always seemed to the donor that he was giving the larger share! He and his wife had found happiness but it hadn't been so easy and they had had to give up a lot and give in a lot before years and tolerance helped them to a better understanding of each other.

Maybe it would be easier for these two. Mary was very unselfish and of a loving generous disposition. Paul seemed as nice a young man as he had ever met. Yet deep in his heart, he could not feel happy to agreeing that they should take Jackie into their lives. It might have been different if they had

already been married some years
. . . but at the start of their life
together . . .

'Perhaps Mrs. Mayhew could go with
you?' he suggested. 'Naturally I should
finance any such arrangement . . .
Jackie is my child after all. I'd have to
come to some arrangement with Paul
about his expenses. Maybe if Mrs.
Mayhew went with you, you would not
be so tied.'

'But, Uncle Tom, I shan't have
anything else to do but look after
Jackie. Paul arranged for Mrs. King's
eldest daughter to come in to do the
rough work. I shall have only the
cooking and shopping to do . . . and
Paul has warned me that he will be
busy. Having Jackie to look after and for
company will help fill my time. Besides,
I'd thought Mrs. Mayhew might stay on
with you, Uncle, as cook-housekeeper.
You cannot manage alone. I asked her
yesterday if she would consider such an
arrangement if you liked the idea and
she said she would.'

'I'll talk it over with Paul after dinner!' her Uncle said at last.

Mary was not present when her Uncle talked the matter over with Paul. She knew nothing of Paul's own private feelings on the matter of Jackie.

'I rather tend to your views, sir!' he had said to her Uncle. 'But on the other hand, Mary isn't like other girls. For one thing, she is completely home-loving. For a second, she always has and always will feel directly responsible for Jackie. I think she would have a deep feeling of guilt if she left Jackie here with Mrs. Mayhew, not because she would think him anything but well cared for, but because she knows her Aunt would not have liked it; would have expected *her* to take care of him. I don't want Mary ever to act against her conscience because of me. And that's not altogether unselfish. You see, I wouldn't want her to blame me if anything went wrong.'

'It is a big step to take, Paul, though not, of course, an irrevocable one. If it didn't work out, we could have Jackie home again.'

'I had thought of that!' Paul said grinning. 'It isn't that I'm not fond of the boy, sir . . . you know that. It's just that . . . well, I'm selfish enough to want Mary all to myself. On the other hand, I do realize that I shall have to leave her alone a lot and he will be company for her . . . I think it's really up to Mary herself. If she can work it out happily for everyone the way she wants, then let's have it that way. That's my view, sir.'

Mary was so radiant with happiness when Paul told her the decision had been reached, that he felt nearly all of his own uncertainty leave him. He loved her so much . . . and her happiness meant more to him than anything in the world. Let her have the boy if it was going to make her eyes shine and her mouth curve so happily in that lovely smile.

He took her in his arms and tried not to think how long the weeks would be before he could make her at last his wife. Her Uncle had suggested six months . . . and that had seemed to him a fair time to wait, out of respect for Mrs. Bradbourne. He could with his finer feelings accept the necessity for this delay even while his whole heart argued fiercely against it and hungered for the girl whom he held in his arms.

14

The honeymoon had been for both Mary and Paul a brief period in their lives when everything was magical and utterly perfect. They had gone to Cornwall where the August sun blazed hot from the blue sky for every day of their fortnight . . . a miracle in itself! The days had been filled with long, lazy hours on the lonely stretch of beach which they had made their private little Paradise. The hours had been filled with laughter and excitement as they rode their surf boards among the Atlantic rollers, or with quiet conversation, hands entwined, as they lay with eyes closed in the sunshine on the golden sands. They returned to their hotel only to eat enormous meals and to sleep. During the evening, they would climb the rocks or go for long walks along the cliffs, always perfect companions for one another, always in sympathy, always deeply, surely and perfectly in love.

For Mary, her initiation into marriage had made the greatest change. When her first shyness and natural reticence had worn off, she had discovered in herself depths she had not believed to be there. In the quiet hours of darkness as she lay in Paul's arms, she marvelled at the wonder of his love-making and at the miracle of her own body responding to him. Paul never let her feel she was just a woman. In his arms, she became a queen, someone who could give him joy and peace and utter content. She had not imagined there could be so perfect a way to make the man she loved so happy. She felt proud and much older and wiser although Paul still teased her by telling her he had been cradle-snatching.

On their last day, they had tried not to think that tomorrow they must leave all this behind them and go back to work! Mary was excited at the thought of returning to their new home . . . the home that had waited so long for them, yet her spirits fell a little when she remembered that Paul would be away a good deal of the day. She had grown so used to having him by her side!

She was filled with resolutions on that drive home. She would never let Paul see she minded taking second place. So confident was she that he would prefer to be with her, she could afford to be generous to her rival . . . his work! She would be the perfect wife . . . understanding, tactful, interested in his job and his patients, answer the telephone for him, help him with his paper work. And she would cook wonderful meals for him and darn his socks and everything that she did for him would be for her own pleasure, too.

Paul, too, was thinking that their honeymoon had ended now. As he drove homewards, his thoughts had turned to his work . . . to various patients whom he had left in Dr. Law's care, of the extra work he would have to tackle to catch up. He knew he would be busy and even while he accepted the demands on his time as part of a doctor's life, he knew he would hate leaving his darling Mary, even for a moment!

He thought, too, of the boy, Jackie. At least Mary would not be alone in the house and miss his company too much. He was suddenly glad for his own sake that Mary had arranged to collect the child on their way home. When she had first told him, he had felt the tiniest spark of jealousy . . . that Mary should want Jackie their first night in their new home. Could she not wait until the next day? he had asked himself. The child would have spent fourteen days alone with Mrs. Mayhew . . . surely another twenty-four hours would not harm him!

But now he felt so supremely confident of Mary's love . . . of her feelings for him and her need of him, that he found he did not mind in the least about Jackie. He knew her heart to be wholly and completely his.

It was late when at last they drew up outside Mary's old home. Mrs. Mayhew opened the door to them, her face full of welcome, but a trifle worried. Mary said quickly:

'Jackie's all right?'

'Oh, yes! He's very well!' the older woman said as they went into the hall. 'But he has been a little ... well, difficult. I think he began to wonder if you were really coming, Mary!'

'Oh, dear!' Mary said, her face clouding. 'Your letters gave no indication of it so I never thought —'

'Well, he wasn't ill, or I would have told you,' Mrs. Mayhew broke in. 'I think he had just been playing up a little, as you know, he does if he can't get his own way. It's been more a question of tantrums. Anyway, I've no doubt he will be quite all right now you are back.'

'He's been spoilt!' Paul said, speaking in a medical capacity and without forethought.

Mary shot him a glance full of reproach.

'Paul, how can you say that? As if one could do too much for a child in Jackie's position.'

Paul bit back the reply that rose to his lips and smiled instead. This was no time to discuss the boy's upbringing.

'Don't let's worry about it now, darling,' he said gently. Then to Mrs. Mayhew: 'He's not in bed yet?'

'Oh, no, Dr. Deal . . . he refused to go to bed and . . . well, I didn't want him over-tired or over-excited before you arrived, so I gave in. He's in his bedroom . . . hat and coat on and suitcase packed. He's ready to leave now.'

Mary was already half way upstairs and a moment later returned with a beaming Jackie. They bade Mrs. Mayhew good-bye and were soon back in the car and driving the few streets to their new home.

Mrs. King's daughter had been in the house all day, cleaning and making up beds and lighting the boiler. As Paul turned the key in the front door, a delicious smell of cooking wafted towards him. He turned to Mary, who held Jackie's hand in hers, and said:

'Let him go a moment, Mary, I want to carry you over the threshold!'

Mary started to smile, but her face clouded as Jackie clung more tightly to her hand and said:

'Won't let go, *won't*!'

'Come on, old chap!' Paul said kindly. 'I'll carry you over the doormat first!'

But Jackie stubbornly refused to let go of Mary's hand and Paul felt his irritation rise.

'Make him let go, Mary!' he said quietly. 'It's only for a moment.'

Mary looked anxiously from Jackie to Paul and back to Jackie as his face screwed up and he started to bawl. But there was an expression in Paul's eyes that made her reach for Jackie's hand with her free one and prise open his fingers. As soon as she was free, Paul bent and lifted her into his arms, but the happiness and pleasure that there might have been in this moment for them both was quite spoilt by the terrible howl that accompanied them as Jackie gave vent to his feelings.

As soon as Paul had put her down, Mary ran back to fetch the boy and was so busy trying to calm him that she did not notice this time the expression on Paul's face as he watched her. There was uneasiness in it, and a little anger, a lot of fear.

Was Mary's maternal instinct stronger than the love she had for him?

Suddenly the frown left his forehead and he shook his head as if to clear it of such thoughts. How childish and stupid it was of him to feel jealous of a child . . . how unworthy!

He picked up Jackie's suitcase and followed his wife and the boy upstairs.

After Jackie was in bed and asleep, Mary became his own girl again . . . the girl he had discovered on their honeymoon. She ran from room to room in their little house, exclaiming at the flowers Mrs. King had arranged for them . . . running to Paul to throw her arms round his neck and hug him as she read from the card beneath one beautiful bowl of roses that they were Paul's gift to her.

She was radiant and glowing with happiness and Paul felt all his confidence in her return. They were going to be so very happy, here in their first home. How wonderful it was to be here and not in digs!

After they had eaten the supper Mrs. King had left in the oven for them, they curled up on the big sofa in the deepening twilight and Mary leant her head on Paul's shoulder and sighed.

'It's all so wonderful, Paul!' she whispered. 'I'm so afraid I shall wake up and find it is all a dream!'

Paul kissed her and she knew that she was not dreaming. If she were, then they were dreams that had come true for always.

'Shall we always be as happy as this?' she asked.

'Always!' Paul told her. 'For as long as we both love each other as we do, how can we not be happy?'

'Nothing can ever come between us now, can it?' Mary said, more as a statement than a question, for the memory of Aunt Ethel and how nearly she had prevented this marriage had come unbidden to her thoughts.

But before Paul could answer her, the phone rang and with a wry smile Paul released her from his arms and stood up.

'There's something that will do its best to part us!' he grinned. '*ça commence*, Mary . . . it begins!'

Laughing, she stood up and squared her shoulders in mock resignation.

'Well, don't let me detain you, Dr. Deal. I'll go and put the kettle on for a cup of tea!'

But there was to be no cup of tea for Paul. The phone call was from Dr. Law to say that if Paul were not too tired, he was urgently needed at a cottage two or three miles away, where a young child had been scalded by a kettle of water.

'I'm about to deliver a baby at the hospital,' Dr. Law said, 'and your replacement is on his way home and I can't reach him. Can you go, Paul?'

With a brief explanation to Mary, Paul hurried into the bedroom to change his shirt and have a wash, and within five minutes he was out of the house and driving away in his car.

'It may mean I'll have to go to the hospital with the child,' he had warned Mary, 'so don't wait up for me, darling. I may be late!'

With a little sigh, Mary drank the tea she had made and went slowly up the stairs to bed.

She was suddenly very tired but she resolved she would not sleep until Paul came home. She would read until she heard the car come back and then run downstairs to welcome him! She had already thought of a hot drink in a thermos and cut some sandwiches which she had carefully rolled in a napkin. Now there was nothing more she could do for him but wait.

When Paul came home three hours later, however, she was fast asleep and did not wake, even when he climbed into bed beside her. He wondered for a moment if he should wake her, and laughing at himself for such selfish thoughts, decided against it. He looked at her for a little while as she lay softly breathing, her fair hair a cloud on the white pillow, the lashes thick and dark on her cheeks. They had lost their pallor and the sun had tanned her to a beautiful golden brown, surprising them both, for with her fair skin, Mary had expected to burn.

'I love her more than anything in the world!' Paul thought, as he switched off the light. Very gently, he put his arm around her, and in her sleep she sighed and moved closer to him. Paul was quite content.

★　★　★

The following days were, Mary found, much as Paul had predicted. He would leave in the morning after breakfast, having already been called to the telephone several times during that meal, and could not tell her for certain if he would be back to lunch. Sometimes he would come in late when her carefully prepared meal would have dried up in the oven and only with the greatest restraint could she refrain from letting him see her disappointment. If he were back for tea, it was often only to be called out again later, or for evening surgery, and at least once a week he was called out in the night. The assistant Dr. Law had engaged while Paul was on holiday had gone back to London and there seemed more than enough work for the two doctors to deal with.

Paul told Mary that Dr. Law had considered taking on a full-time assistant and that he had agreed. The practice could afford it financially and it would greatly ease the pressure of work.

The trouble at the moment was to find the right man. Meanwhile, there was no way to avoid the long hours of work.

As Paul had anticipated, Mary turned to Jackie for companionship and the days passed quickly enough. There was breakfast to clear away, the shopping or washing or ironing to do in the morning while Mrs. King's daughter cleaned the house. After lunch, there was Jackie's walk and then home for tea; his bedtime and Paul's supper to get. And all through the day the telephone rang and Mary took messages for Paul and felt that in this way she was helping him a little in his work.

She was a little concerned to see how tired Paul looked at the end of the day. The summer had continued to be hot and sultry and Mary knew from her own feelings as well as Jackie's how irritable the heat could make one, and was not surprised if Paul was sometimes a little short with her. Once or twice, she found herself answering back in like tone and then stopped herself, realizing they had been about to quarrel. Then she would go into Paul's arms and he would be telling her how sorry he was to have snapped at her and all would be right again.

But there came a day towards the very end of summer when Mary did not bite back the retort that came to her lips, and they did quarrel. It had really begun some days ago when Paul suggested they should snatch two days at the week-end to run down to his home.

Mary had readily agreed.

'It would be lovely, Paul darling. Can you really get away?'

'I think so. Of course, it means leaving late on the Friday night and coming back at dawn on the Monday. That would give us Saturday and Sunday clear.'

'But, Paul, if we're to get down by Jackie's bedtime, we'll have to leave on Friday afternoon.'

The inevitable telephone call had interrupted the discussion, which had not been resumed until the following day. Then Paul said:

'Look, darling, about this trip home . . . I think the long car ride may be a bit much for Jackie . . . it's nearly two hundred miles, you know.'

'But I can't leave him!' Mary said. 'You're not suggesting that?'

Paul's voice rose a little.

'Well, why not, Mary? We can take him round to your Uncle's house and Mrs. Mayhew can look after him.'

It was a perfectly reasonable suggestion and had it not been for the tone of Paul's voice, Mary might have acted otherwise. But she was tired, too, and always quick in defence of Jackie she said:

'Don't you want him to come, Paul? After all, we *could* take him, couldn't we? He'd enjoy the change of air. You know he hasn't had a holiday this year. Besides, your Mother told me she'd like me to take him down when I could.'

'It isn't that at all!' Paul said

patiently. 'It's just that we shall have very little time and unless we leave on the Friday, it isn't worth going at all.'

'And you can't get away Friday afternoon?'

'You know I can't, Mary. Friday evening is my surgery.'

'Couldn't Dr. Law do it for you?'

'I dare say, but I don't intend to ask him,' Paul answered, his irritation getting the better of him. Why should Mary choose this moment to be so unreasonable. 'He had a lot of extra work to do while we were on our honeymoon and he'll be working overtime on Saturday and Sunday. In fact, if he hadn't himself suggested the week-end, I would never have dreamt of asking for it. I did so because I thought you looked a bit tired.'

'Well, please don't act against your duty for my sake!'

Even as she said the words, Mary knew she was being childish, but she could not this time control herself.

'Oh, don't be so silly!' The words

came out before Paul could stop them. He saw Mary's face whiten and was tempted to apologize, but her next words stopped him.

'It's quite clear you'd rather go without Jackie. Well, I have my duty, too, and *I* am not going without him. He needs the holiday more than either of us.'

'Nonsense!' Paul said angrily. 'He's as fit and well as he could be, and you know it. Don't be so silly about him, Mary. You spoil the child.'

'You said that once before!' Mary said through tight lips. 'I don't think so. You just don't understand Jackie!'

'And that is nonsense, too!' Paul said quickly. 'I understand him a good deal better than you do, Mary. You're nearly as obsessed with him as that Aunt of yours!'

It was the wind to fan the flames and instantly their quarrel became hot and violent.

'You know damn well Jackie would be quite all right with Mrs. Mayhew.

You're just trying to be difficult!' Paul flung at her.

'That isn't the point. You're just using the long drive as an excuse not to take him.'

'All right! Why shouldn't I take you away by yourself? You're my wife, aren't you? Haven't I a right to wish to be alone with you?'

'Alone? With all your family? Don't make excuses, Paul.'

'Confound it, I'm not making excuses!' Paul was nearly shouting now. 'I don't want to take him . . . it isn't worth the bother and trouble for such a short while.'

'So he's a bother and trouble now?' Mary said quietly, her mouth hard. 'I'd tried to see that he didn't bother or trouble you, Paul. I see I've failed.'

'Oh, for goodness' sake!' Paul cried. 'This is too childish. I didn't say he was a nuisance, did I?'

'Didn't you?'

'No, I didn't! But I'll say it now. The whole idea is too much trouble and certainly a nuisance. Let's forget about it!'

He swung on his heel and walked out of the room, banging the door behind him.

Mary buried her face in her hands and burst into tears. Her anger had left her now and she was aghast at the scene which had just ensued, terrified by Paul's abrupt departure. How could they have quarrelled so dreadfully!

Within five minutes, she had reached the conclusion that it had all been of her making. She *had* perhaps been unreasonable about Jackie. He could quite well go to Mrs. Mayhew. It was just Paul's attitude that had struck her as being so . . . unkind. She had been aghast to hear the angry tone of his voice and she was desperately hurt. Whatever Paul thought about her behaviour with Jackie . . . or about the advisability of taking him to Devon or not, he had no cause to speak to her that way!

Injured feelings prevented her from

doing what she really wanted to do deep in her heart . . . to go to him and ask him to forgive her for being childish and contrary and to make up their quarrel quickly. But she was proud and would not make the first move.

Paul, too, was wishing to put an end to the thoroughly unpleasant atmosphere which followed their quarrel. He felt that he had said more than he intended about the boy, but then he had momentarily lost his temper and Mary certainly provoked him. Deep down inside, he knew he was jealous of Mary's consideration for the boy. If she were only a little more reasonable in her attitude to the child, he would not have felt so intolerant. But there was no question about the fact that she spoiled him. Jackie had been thoroughly spoiled since he was a tiny baby. And Paul believed that he was sensible enough to know just how far he could go; know how to work himself into a state of hysteria if necessary to get his own way.

But how could he possibly say all this

to Mary when she was blind to anything but the child's good points. It was this blind spot that so got on his nerves. In everything else, Mary was as reasonable as she could be . . . always willing to discuss . . . to listen to his point of view and she respected his opinion and judgment as a doctor as well as a man. But he knew without trying it out that she would argue hotly in Jackie's defence if he breathed any form of criticism.

For two or three days longer, it was deadlock between them . . . neither would make a move to be the first to apologize and the week-end was still undecided and hung between their stilted conversations like an unhappy cloud.

It was Thursday evening before Mary capitulated. She could not bear the tension between herself and Paul to go on any longer. At the same time, she was not yet ready to say she was sorry. When he came in to supper, she announced in a cold tone:

'I've spoken to Mrs. Mayhew and she will take Jackie home tomorrow afternoon after his walk. Uncle Tom will be glad to have him for the week-end.'

It needed no more for Paul to be on his feet and round to Mary's chair. As his arms went round her, she gave a little cry and burst into tears.

'Don't, darling, don't!' Paul whispered. 'I can't bear to see you crying. Mary, dearest, darling, don't. I've been a brute . . . I'm terribly sorry, Sweet. We'll take the boy if it means so much to you!'

Even as she gloried in Paul's capitulation and the pleasure of ending their horrible frightening quarrel, Mary felt a tiny moment of irritation. Paul's offer to take Jackie came too late. Had he meant it, or was it merely a pretty safe suggestion since she had made her plans for Jackie to go to his father?

But her doubt lasted only a moment and then, angry with herself for thinking such nasty thoughts when Paul was being so sweet to her, she in her turn asked him to forgive her.

It was on the tip of Paul's tongue to take this opportunity to discuss Jackie, but fortunately he did not. His thoughts on the question of the child's behaviour he shelved for some future date. Jackie was spoilt and sooner or later Mary must be made to see it. Meanwhile, maybe Nature would take a hand in things. If Mary had a child of her own, her attention and time, and above all her maternal affections, would have to be divided. That was the obvious and perfect solution!

Quite oblivious to his thoughts, Mary nestled happily in his arms and told herself she would never never quarrel with Paul again.

15

But unhappily, the week-end at Paul's home did not take place. On Friday morning, two of Paul's patients were down with a form of summer 'flu, and by the afternoon, there had been five more telephone calls asking the doctor to call as soon as he could. Noting the symptoms on the message pad, Mary realized with the medical knowledge she was acquiring that it looked as if they were in for an epidemic of the 'flu. She began to wonder if their trip might be put off.

When Paul returned at tea-time, his face was creased with disappointment.

'I'm terribly sorry, dearest . . . this means we can't go, of course!'

'Oh, Paul!' Mary cried, although she had been expecting it.

He kissed her and gave her a tired smile.

'I warned you being a doctor's wife would have disappointments like this,' he reminded her.

Mary squared her shoulders.

'I know, darling. But it does seem such a shame . . . ' most of all that they should have had that horrible quarrel for nothing.

'Jackie still here?' Paul asked, as he sat down to drink the tea Mary had ready for him.

'No! I left him with Mrs. Mayhew this afternoon.'

Mary frowned, remembering how Jackie had howled when she left. She nearly spoke of it to Paul but he looked so tired and disappointed that she decided not to bother him just now with her own worries.

'I suppose you'll have to go out again?' she asked, as he scanned the message pad. 'I'll go round and collect Jackie while you're away.'

Paul looked up.

'I wouldn't do that, darling . . . I mean, it might upset him to

285

change plans again.'

Mary's lips tightened.

'But there's no point leaving him there now we aren't going, Paul.'

Paul looked down unseeingly at his teacup.

'I didn't mean that. But for the last two days you've prepared the boy for spending the week-end with his father and Mrs. Mayhew. I don't think it's fair to him to bring him back now.'

In spite of her decision, Mary now told him about Jackie's screams when she had left.

'So you see,' she finished, 'it isn't fair to him to leave him when it isn't necessary.'

'Look, Mary!' Paul said, speaking carefully. 'You must try to see this from the point of view of what is best for Jackie. If you collect him this evening, he'll think to himself that he has only to howl for you and he gets his way. Next time, when you can't collect him, he won't understand.'

There was reason in what Paul said,

but somewhere in Mary's heart lay a new distrust of Paul's motives. She could not help but wonder if he *wanted* Jackie out of the way . . . was using his arguments merely to get his own way! After all, Paul had been the one to suggest that they took Jackie to live with them. He couldn't go back on it now. It must be one thing or the other . . . either Jackie lived with them or with his father and Mrs. Mayhew. Surely Paul realized that she wouldn't have left home . . . got married so soon, if Jackie were not going to live with her?

Could Paul be regretting his offer to have Jackie? She could not understand why, if it were so. The boy always behaved very well whenever Paul was with him, and more often than not, he was in bed asleep by the time Paul came home, wanting Mary to himself. He had never 'got in Paul's way' and she, herself, could see no reason why Paul should have changed his mind. Nonetheless, it did look as if he were taking every chance he could to get

Jackie out of the house.

'You're very quiet!' Paul broke in on her thoughts.

'I was just . . . thinking . . . ' Mary said evasively. 'All right, Paul . . . I'll leave Jackie where he is if that's what you want.'

Paul's irritation rose quickly to the surface.

'It isn't what I want!' he said, striving to keep his voice calm. 'It's just that I consider it best for Jackie.'

Mary looked at Paul and bit back the accusation that rose to her lips. She could not bear to quarrel with him again . . . and she had no right to distrust Paul's motives. He loved her and he was the kindest and most wonderful husband in the world! He was unfailingly patient and thoughtful and tender with her. How could she doubt for a single moment that he was being selfish or unkind about Jackie?

Her love for Paul was complete and absolute. Her love for Jackie was something quite apart in her mind and yet in some strange way the two seemed to be warring together within her heart. What had happened to start this conflict of emotions? She must never never let anything happen to spoil her relationship with Paul.

Mary was too young and inexperienced to see that it was going to require a good deal of tact and clever handling to divide her loyalties between the man she had married and the boy she had taken into her care. Paul was not of a jealous disposition, but he was beginning to resent what he called Mary's 'blind spot' where Jackie was concerned. In her eyes, Jackie could do no wrong. If he were wilful or bad-tempered or sullen, she excused him by saying he was not well . . . it was one of his 'bad days'. She never punished him. He had his own way in everything; even to what he wished to eat and what time he went to bed. Mary ran her household round Jackie's requirements and while they did not in fact conflict with Paul's . . . for he had no regular routine or wish for one . . . he could see that it was thoroughly bad for the boy. Jackie was by no means as abnormal as Mary believed. He had tried once to explain to her that his was a case of arrested development. His brain, in so far as it had developed, was fairly normal . . . and these fits he had occasionally were really brought on by the child himself in an effort to get his own way. But Mary would not believe it. She reiterated that she had known Jackie far longer than Paul . . . since he was a tiny baby; that he had always had these bad days and there was nothing for it but to be patient.

Paul did not agree. His resentment was not of the child himself, but of Mary's treatment of him. But he had not admitted this even to himself in so many words.

Mary was not foolish. She had a great deal of common sense and Paul, thinking over it carefully, could see that her feelings for Jackie, and her treatment of him, were something she had absorbed in her early childhood from her Aunt. It was natural that the little girl should believe what her Aunt told her about Jackie's welfare and moods and the way he should be treated. And when one has grown up with a belief, however misplaced, it is by no means easy to assert an adult commonsense attitude in direct conflict with those deep-rooted convictions.

That night, when he held her in his arms, he told her that he would like a child.

Mary was at first a little surprised, then happy and finally a little dismayed. She would like a baby . . . Paul's child. It would be the perfect result of their union; the right and normal outcome for the glory of their love-making. And yet . . . well, how could she cope with a baby just now? Jackie combined with the housekeeping and her acting as a kind of secretary for Paul made up a full-time job.

She forgot that his mother had done all these things and borne six children.

'Oh, Paul . . . I would like a baby . . . ' she said at last . . . 'but not just yet . . . let's wait a little while.'

Paul's emotions were mixed. They were, after all, very newly married . . . it was only four months since their wedding! And Mary was still very young. If it were only these things . . . but he felt instinctively that it was not.

'Why not yet?' he asked after a moment's silence.

'Well . . . I . . . I . . . Paul, I just don't feel I really *want* a baby now.'

'I think you would . . . when you carried it!' Paul said. 'You love children, don't you, darling? And your own baby . . . ours . . . '

She felt her heart weaken with tenderness . . . and then fear took hold of her again . . . and that unbidden, unfair mistrust of Paul. What was his motive? Was he going to suggest that once she had a child of her own she would not want Jackie here any more?

'Paul!' the words were wrung from

her. 'Don't you love Jackie?'

Paul's eyes stared into the darkness.

'Of course I'm devoted to him, you know that!' he said carefully. 'But he isn't our child, Mary . . . yours and mine. I don't quite see what he has to do with this.'

'Only that it wouldn't be fair to make differences between Jackie and our children . . . ' Mary thought, but did not say. Yet after all, how could she expect Paul to love Jackie as she did. He had only known him a short while . . . not even a year. And in time he would feel differently, she was sure of it . . . or wanted to be sure of it. Lying in the darkness, she thought the matter over carefully. If they had a baby right away, Paul would be so absorbed in it that he would never take time to really get to know and love Jackie.

It never once occurred to Mary that she might not be doing the right thing to take her responsibilities for her cousin so seriously. They were natural feelings . . . part of her being, and she did not try to analyse them. But her Uncle had warned her that married life was not always as easy as it seemed when one was 'courting' and that it would make things more difficult for them if they had trouble over the child. Mary had never conceived it possible that they should have 'trouble' over Jackie, and even now that they had quarrelled quite seriously over him, she had not once believed that she was perhaps being unfair to Paul. Paul had always been so loving and understanding, so completely in sympathy with her, that she could not . . . would not believe he was jealous or resented the child being there.

The misunderstanding that lay between them was not because they had ceased to love one another . . . nor had they ceased *trying* to see the other's point of view. It was there because each had these inner convictions and they were so deep-rooted that they could not see why the other did not see the question of Jackie in their own way.

Paul worried only because he felt Mary spoilt the child; that she gave too much of herself for the child's good or her own. Mary worried because she suspected Paul did not really love the child and was regretting his suggestion that Jackie live with them.

Now the field of misunderstanding had spread. Mary wanted a baby . . . really wanted one, just as much as Paul did. But she put Jackie first in her mind and misled Paul into thinking she was not, after all, as keen to raise a family as he was. He was both disappointed and hurt and a new barrier rose between them, each wishing to remove it and yet neither quite sure what they could do.

When, two months later, Mary found herself pregnant in spite of Paul's promises that it would not happen, she felt he had deliberately 'cheated' to get his own way. While deep down within her, she was thrilled at the knowledge Dr. Law had given her, her mind fought against the natural instinct and she put off telling Paul until he had guessed at the truth for himself.

He was desperately hurt that she had not told him as soon as she suspected the truth . . . or at least when she was sure. Dr. Law, respecting Mary's request, had told Paul nothing, waiting for Paul to speak first.

'It makes me look rather a fool!' he said to Mary when she admitted the truth. 'Dr. Law must have been wondering this month why I hadn't spoken of it. *Why* didn't you tell me?'

Mary had not been feeling at all well. She had been very sick in the mornings and sometimes in the evenings and it had been quite difficult to conceal the fact from Paul even as long as this. She knew it was stupid of her to try and hide it from him and yet, perversely, she had continued to do so for as long as she could.

'I presumed you must have guessed for yourself,' she said coldly. 'After all, I didn't arrive in this condition by myself!'

Paul looked at her amazed. Was this his soft, sweet loving Mary . . . the girl he had fallen in love with? What had happened to them? Why had this strange barrier grown between them? Where had he gone wrong? Most of all, what could Mary mean by her last remark?

'I don't understand you,' he said quietly.

'Don't you? Had you forgotten you promised me you would see I didn't start a baby for at least six months?'

Paul suddenly laughed. So that was the trouble!

'Well, for goodness' sake, darling, even the best of people make mistakes . . . I mean, I did my part faithfully, but these things can happen nonetheless.' He saw her white, drawn face, and his expression softened. He held out his arms to her.

'Dearest, don't let's quarrel about this. I'm so very happy at the news . . . even if I do wish I'd known sooner. Be a little pleased, too!'

She went into his arms then, partly because she so longed for everything to be right between them again, partly because she was tired and did not feel too well and she wanted to be petted and comforted. She cried a little but would not admit any pleasure in the baby . . . she would not give in the whole way.

Their relationship took a turn for the better as the next three months passed. Paul was sweet and kind and so spontaneously glad about the baby that Mary felt her own behaviour to have been childish and small in comparison. She felt fitter and, though a little tired, had ceased to be irritable because of her condition, and her love for Paul took on a new aspect.

There were long letters from Paul's family in Devon and, as Mary had hoped, it was possible for them to go down together for a few days at the New Year. Here in the friendly, loving atmosphere of Paul's home, with its poignant memories of last year, Mary became heart and soul Paul's 'girl' again.

Jean was home and she and Mary spent many hours together 'gossiping' and established a friendship which was to last their lifetime. Jean confided in Mary that she was at last contemplating settling down with young Edwin . . . or at least to consent to an engagement.

Mary was delighted and felt sure Mrs. Deal would be, too, for they all liked the young man and felt, if anything, that he was too good and too unselfish with Jean! But Jean disarmed them all by admitting it was so, and she privately confided in Mary that this was the one reason she still hesitated.

'I know I can be very self-willed and dictatorial!' she said. 'And I value my independence. Edwin says I can carry on with my job if I want and live just as if I were still a bachelor girl. But in my heart, I know it wouldn't make him really happy. I think he believes if he gives me long enough rope I'll run myself out and want to settle down to domesticity eventually. In a way, I do now, but I'm afraid I'll get the better of Edwin in every argument we ever have. He's far too good to me and I'll take advantage of it!'

Mary laughed.

'But surely not if you know the position!' she said to Jean.

'It isn't always easy to curb your faults, even when you know you're indulging them,' Jean said. 'I've got a horrible temper and I don't control it . . . not with Edwin, because he always forgives me.'

'You mean, you've lost your temper with Edwin *already*?' Mary asked in surprise.

Jean laughed.

'Well, why not? If we're going to disagree, we might as well find out now as later. Mary, don't you and Paul ever have different opinions about anything?'

Mary felt the colour in her cheeks. Loyalty to Paul prevented her telling Jean about those differences but she did admit that they weren't always in agreement.

'I'd begun to think you both quite unnatural!' Jean teased. Then they talked of the baby and Mary's last doubts about her own feelings in the matter disappeared. She was utterly content (as Paul had told her she would be) to be carrying a child . . . her child and Paul's. She had momentarily completely forgotten Jackie.

It was unfortunate that Paul should have been forced to bring him into the conversation again soon after their return home and in the way he felt necessary to speak. Mary always pushed the heavy invalid push-chair round the Park in the afternoons when she took Jackie for his walk. Paul had sometimes seen her struggling up or down the steps with the boy still in the pram and been tempted to tell her to let Jackie walk. He could quite well do so when he chose! But he had refrained from a suggestion that might be in the form of criticism of her treatment of the boy, knowing how touchy she was about him and how callous she thought him, Paul!

But now it was too much to see her pushing and struggling, and as a doctor he could not allow her to overdo things at this stage of her pregnancy. As tactfully as he could, he told her she must give up the pram pushing and let Jackie take his afternoon walk on his feet.

'He is quite capable of walking to the gardens and back,' he said. 'And it might even work off some of his energy.'

'But he always goes in the pram!' Mary said stupidly. Except in really bad weather or if he were ill, Jackie had been pushed out in the pram every afternoon of his life.

'Well, I realize that!' Paul replied carefully. 'But you can ask Dr. Law if you do not wish to accept my view as a doctor . . . Jackie can walk without it doing him any harm. And pushing him might well harm you, darling. You don't want to lose the baby, do you?'

She did not. Yet instinctively she

stiffened in Jackie's defence.

'I know you think he only plays up, Paul, but he isn't like other children . . . he tires easily.'

'Then don't go quite so far,' Paul said reasonably. 'Just take him for a short walk.'

'But he likes the gardens . . . he can play there with the other children,' Mary argued.

'Well, if he likes it enough, he'll let you walk him all the way there!' Paul retorted. 'Anyway, Mary, it is quite out of the question that *you* should go on pushing him. Let Mrs. Mayhew take him if you insist he shall remain in a pram!'

He knew his feelings had been badly expressed when he saw the light flash into Mary's eyes.

'Mrs. Mayhew has enough to do keeping house for Uncle Tom. She only has the afternoon to herself. Besides, Jackie is my responsibility.'

'Not entirely!' Paul argued, in spite of his knowledge that he was only making matters worse. 'You must not forget that Uncle Tom is his father, and it may interest you to know, Mary, that he wanted us to get a Nanny for Jackie and to let him pay for it. Personally, I think it is an excellent suggestion now the baby is coming. You will be too busy to manage both of them. A baby can be very exacting, you know.'

Mary's lips tightened and her face was dead-white as she listened to Paul's words. So she had been right after all . . . Paul wanted this baby to separate her from Jackie. He was using his unborn child as a weapon.

'*If* we get a Nanny, it will be for the baby,' she said through clenched teeth. 'I shall continue to look after Jackie as I think best.'

Paul tried to make allowances for her condition and failed. He knew himself to be thoroughly stupid but he could not hold back his words.

'You have not just yourself to consider, Mary. You happen to be married to me and since you are my wife, don't you think you owe me some say in the matter?'

'I don't interfere with your work!' Mary cried childishly. 'Why should you interfere with mine?'

Paul gave an exasperated sigh. Then common sense overcame his annoyance and he realized that Mary *was* young, not always very tactful, and he *must* make allowances for the fact that she was tired and overwrought. But how could he make her look after herself properly so that she did not get overtired when she was going to be so stubborn about Jackie.

For the first time, Paul began to feel his irritation spill over towards the child himself. He knew he was being unfair and tried to keep the thought at bay. Nevertheless, it was beyond his powers not to admit to himself that but for Jackie's presence in the house, he and Mary would be perfectly happy. They never quarrelled over anything else.

Inexperienced as she was with dealing with men . . . or a husband,

Mary was ignorant of the fact that every time she argued with Paul about Jackie, she made matters more difficult not only for him, but for herself. The very thing she believed to be true . . . Paul's wish to separate her from the boy . . . was coming about through *her* behaviour. But she could not see it. Stubbornly, she continued to push Jackie in the heavy pram to and from the gardens. Each day, she felt a little more exhausted by the effort, each day became a little more certain that Paul was right, but she would not give way. Paul watched her in silence and with a deep uneasiness, knowing himself powerless to prevent what he felt sure must result.

And in January, Mary lost her baby.

16

For a few days, Mary was quite seriously ill. She lay in the hospital bed, ashen-faced, silent and very shocked. It had been a terrible experience for her, and deep down in her heart she was all too conscious of where the blame lay. She knew she had deliberately disobeyed Paul's advice, a doctor's advice, in order to sustain her own pride. Now she had lost her baby . . .

Often, tears would run quietly down her cheeks. The young Irish nurse pretended not to notice them and tried to cheer Mary up with amusing talk of other patients or her hospital experiences told with humour and friendliness. Miscarriages nearly always resulted in acute depression of the patient and she was not very greatly concerned; nor was Dr. Law, who attended Mary. But Paul saw beneath the surface and knew that Mary was suffering in her mind as well as in her body.

He had been to see her several times a day. Free as he was to move about the hospital at all hours of the day or night, he spent the first few days in and out of her room. But always she turned her head away on the pillow and she would not speak to him unless there were someone else present and then only to whisper 'yes' or 'no'. When he had tried to take her in his arms, to kiss her, he had felt her body taut beneath his touch and she had turned her face quickly away from his so that his lips touched only her cheek.

His emotions were confused and ever-changing. Only pity and tenderness filled his heart when he went to her first. But as she maintained her frigid silence, he felt irritation take hold of him and a certain sense of injustice. Mary could hardly blame him for what had happened! And she was showing no consideration for his feelings, his disappointment; no gratitude for his quick forgiveness, his tenderness, his sympathy. He could almost believe that she had meant things to be this way.

Yet every time he opened the door of her room and saw her, white-faced and with those enormous violet shadows beneath her eyes, her body seeming painfully thin and shrunken under the white counterpane, his heart weakened again in love and tenderness and he would try yet another time to get close to her.

Mary began to dread Paul's visits. She sensed his pity, his sympathy . . . and his forgiveness was a difficult thing to accept. She knew it was all *her* fault and yet that terrible pride would not permit her to give way. Sometimes she longed desperately to fling herself into his arms, to sob out her own deep disappointment and unhappiness, her terrible feeling of loss; even to tell him of the guilt that lay always in her mind. Had she taken Paul's advice, her baby might still be alive. She had killed her child ... his. Beneath his kindness and tenderness he must hate her.

There lay the root of the trouble. Mary could no longer believe in Paul's love because she had grown to hate herself for the wrong she had done him ... and their child. She could not bring herself to accept his sympathy, his forgiveness or his kindness in place of the love that had once existed ... still existed if she had only been able to see it.

Jackie had gone home and Mrs. Mayhew was caring for him. Mary's Uncle, when he called in to see her, told her he was quite happy and had settled down well.

'Don't you think it would be a good plan to leave him for a while?' he suggested. 'You won't be feeling up to much when you get back and you can have a good rest.'

'Did Paul ask you to say that?' Mary said through tight lips. Her Uncle looked at her in surprise.

'Why no, he didn't!' he said truthfully.

'You promise?'

'But of course!' he said immediately, and then added thoughtfully: 'Look, Mary, if you and Paul have had any disagreements about Jackie, I cannot permit Jackie to live with you. I remember warning both of you that it might not work out. Jackie is my child and he is perfectly all right at home with me and Mrs. Mayhew to care for him. You have no responsibilities to him and there is no *need* for you to have him.'

Tears sprang to Mary's eyes, tears of weakness and frustration.

'But I want him!' she said childishly. 'And now when I get home I'll want him more than ever. I don't want time to think about . . . about . . .'

She broke off, sobbing quietly.

Her Uncle privately resolved to have a good long talk with Paul. Meanwhile he said firmly:

'Your marriage should come before

anything else, Mary. Don't ever forget that.'

'But it could have worked . . . it could!' Mary cried, admitting thereby that it had not . . . 'if only Paul had wanted it, too. But he offered to have Jackie to live with us and then behaves as if he doesn't want him! It isn't fair!'

She was so distressed that her Uncle forbore to say anything more to her now. He patted her hand and said he would be in to see her the next day, and left her alone.

Mary cried into her pillow . . . feeling some relief in these tears. It was so much easier to blame someone else and she had all but talked herself into thinking that in a roundabout way this *had* been Paul's fault. Had he not been so anxious to get rid of Jackie, she would never have been so determined to have her own way with him, and then . . . then . . .

The door opened and Paul came in. He no longer tried to kiss her but stood stiffly by the bed.

312

'Dr. Law says you can come home tomorrow. I spoke to Mrs. King and she says her daughter can stay a few nights so you can take it easy. How are you feeling?'

Mary had been up for an hour before tea and had felt terribly weak and wobbly on her legs. But she would not say so to Paul. She said briefly:

'Quite all right, thank you.'

Paul bit his lip. This could not go on. No couple could live together in this atmosphere! Was there no way he could break down Mary's reserve, or whatever it was that made her behave as she did?

He sat down beside the bed and looking down at his long tapering fingers, said softly:

'We'll make a fresh start, shall we, darling?'

Mary started to speak and then closed her lips. She wanted more than anything in the world to turn to Paul now and tell him 'Yes, yes, yes!' But she could not . . . not until the question of Jackie was resolved once and for all.

313

'Uncle Tom suggested Jackie live with him!' she said at last. 'Is that what you want, Paul?'

She waited anxiously for his reply. On it rested not only Jackie's future, but hers, and Paul's. If he showed now that he had no real love for Jackie, then she would know that she had been right in suspecting him of trying to get Jackie out of the way.

Paul hesitated. He knew deep in his heart that it was what he wanted . . . at least, what he wanted for himself. *If only Mary wanted it, too!* But he didn't wish to make her unhappy, or to go back on the promise he had made her before they were married. If only this baby had lived . . . then Mary might not feel the need for Jackie as a substitute, for he was convinced now that she was translating her need for Jackie into the boy's need for her. As far as he could see, Jackie was quite happy in Mrs. Mayhew's care. It seemed so futile for Mary to behave the way she did when it was not even necessary!

'I don't know!' he said at last. 'We . . . we don't always agree about him, do we? Personally, I am convinced that what Jackie really needs is school. I am aware you don't agree with me. It . . . it makes things rather difficult when we differ in our opinion about the child.'

Mary listened with a sinking heart.

'Perhaps we didn't really know each other very well, you and I!' she said tightly. 'Maybe we should have found ourselves disagreeing about . . . about . . . '

'Our own child? No, I don't think so, Mary. You see, we would have grown up together with him . . . decided each point as it came along . . . when he went to school, where, how late he stayed up or what time he went to bed. You have a rigid set of beliefs about Jackie that allow no room for my opinions. I think I can see things less emotionally than you where Jackie is concerned. I . . . I think he needs school and more discipline. You don't

315

agree with me because you hold your Aunt's views about him.'

Paul spoke reasonably, from his heart. He was glad that at last Mary was prepared to discuss Jackie with him. He did not realize that she was only trying to get at his feelings for the boy. He was a little surprised when she said again:

'*Do you want him back to live with us?*'

'Well, I think he would be better in the end away from *you*!' he said. 'You give in to him too much . . . you're too kind to him, Mary.'

Mary's heart was beating at double its pace. Beneath the sheets, her hands were trembling. She played her last card.

'If Jackie lives with Uncle Tom, then I shall go back to live with them!' she said.

Paul stared at her in amazement.

'You . . . *what?*'

His surprise and the sudden fear that shot through him at the unimagined thought of losing Mary, made him angry.

'I never heard anything so silly, Mary

. . . or so childish. You're my wife! You can't just walk out like that . . . because we happen to disagree about Jackie!'

'We can't go on disagreeing, can we? You always knew how much I loved Jackie, and when my Aunt died, I knew she would never rest in peace unless he was in my care. I thought you understood that when I married you.'

Paul was quiet and tense. He said slowly:

'Are you trying to tell me that if it had come to the point where you had had to choose between Jackie and me, you would not have married me?'

It was not really what Mary meant, or felt. She knew deep in her heart that she *would* have married Paul because she loved him so desperately. But she could in all truth say that she would not have married him when she did.

'I see!' Paul commented. 'Then it is quite clear to me, Mary, that we ought not to have been married at all. You don't begin to know the meaning of the word love, or to understand the meaning of marriage. I thought I had married a woman but I find after all that I married a child. Maybe you should go home . . . and grow up a little first!'

Because he was so desperately hurt, he said far more than he intended and now, unable to take it back, he got up and left the room.

Mary turned her face into the pillow and gave way to the deep shaking sobs that welled up from her torn heart.

★ ★ ★

'Surely you can make her understand, sir?' Paul said to Mary's Uncle as they sat over their coffee that evening. 'It seems so terrible that we should be 'quarrelling' over something that really isn't vital in our marriage.'

'The trouble as I see it is that it has assumed a vital aspect to Mary!' the older man said thoughtfully. 'She has always been devoted to Jackie, ever since she was a tiny girl. Personally I

318

think she . . . she was permitted to spend too much of her time and thought on him. It might have been better for her to have gone to boarding school, to University, to have been away from home more. But I left the domestic arrangements to my wife and she thought she was acting wisely for both the children. You know, it wasn't easy for Ethel; she felt Jackie's accident so keenly, and the consequences affected her more even than I realized . . . until . . . until just before she died. I . . . I guessed what . . . what she said to Mary when she came back from her visit to your people engaged to you. At least, I have a very good idea that she was responsible for Mary's abrupt change of heart about you! But one has to make allowances for . . . for her behaviour.'

'I understand!' Paul said quietly, seeing Tom Bradbourne's distress. 'Don't let's talk about it!'

'But you see, I believe Mary's attitude to be a kind of reflection of her

319

Aunt's. She was always a very impressionable and imaginative little girl.'

'She says she'll come back to live with you if Jackie stays here!' Paul said wearily. 'I can't believe she means it!'

'Perhaps she doesn't. I don't know what to suggest, Paul. Personally, I agree with you. I always thought you would be ill-advised to have the boy to live with you. He is quite all right here with Mrs. Mayhew. Of course, he misses Mary, but he'll get used to it in time.'

'That's what I think!' Paul said eagerly. 'It isn't that I'm not fond of Jackie . . . I am. But Mary and I always seem to be disagreeing about what is best for him. And her behaviour when I asked her not to go on pushing Jackie round in that heavy pram was . . . well, stupid and tragic. I think if I had said nothing at all, she might have given it up of her own accord. But because I asked her, she went on . . . and we lost the baby.'

'You cannot be feeling very kindly

towards her yourself, Paul!' the older man suggested. 'You wanted the baby, didn't you?'

'Yes!' Paul said. 'But there will be others. I love Mary ... and I'll do anything to make her happy that is for *her* good. I don't think it is good for her to go on looking after the boy. That's really what I wanted to tell you, sir.'

'And I agree! But what is to be done, Paul? I cannot refuse to have her live here if she wishes. It is her home and I stand in place of her father.'

'But you might reason with her, sir. I think if she would only give me a chance, I could make her love me again!'

'I'll do my best!' Tom Bradbourne said. 'But I'm not very good at this sort of thing ... not quite in my line! Besides, I don't believe she has stopped loving you, my boy. I think she'll get over it in time.'

But Paul was not quite so sure. He had begun to doubt the quality of Mary's love. She had so often behaved childishly with him that he wondered now if her emotions for him were really as mature as he had always believed. He did not stop to consider that it was Mary's innocence and sometimes child-like behaviour that had first so attracted him to her. Now he was married, Mary was his wife, and he expected her to have 'grown-up' in the short while since their wedding.

He fetched Mary home from the hospital the following morning. There were bunches of flowers in her bedroom and in the drawing-room, carefully chosen and not too skilfully arranged by him as a welcome home. But Mary appeared not to notice them. She spoke only when spoken to and Paul knew that the barrier between them was not to be easily broken down. He said nothing more to her about the question of Jackie's return, waiting for her to speak first.

Mary was tortured by her own feelings. She had seen the flowers . . . realized that Paul was trying to please her, but her heart hardened. If he imagined he was getting his own way about Jackie he was wrong. She had meant what she said . . . that if Jackie stayed with her Uncle, she would go, too. What she really felt was that if Paul did not love her enough to let her have Jackie, she would prefer not to have to go on living with him as his wife. It was no longer Jackie, himself, who was in question . . . but Paul's love for her.

Alone in the house while Paul was working, she got up and wandered into the little room where she had started to prepare for their baby. Tears came weakly to her eyes again as she folded away the tiny knitted garments. Her pain was almost unbearable. She had wanted the baby as much as Paul had and now she might never have a child of her own to hold in her arms and to nurse.

Everywhere she went in the house seemed to remind her of her own guilt and her loss. The silence became oppressive and she began to panic. With sudden determination, she went back to her bedroom and reached for a suitcase and began to pack.

Her intention was to go to her Uncle's house. She knew instinctively that he would welcome her . . . ask no questions. But as she snapped the locks over the few clothes she had packed, she changed her mind. She would go away . . . right away . . . give herself time to think over her life and her future. She no longer wanted to see her Uncle or Jackie or Paul.

Mary stopped downstairs and went to the desk . . . her desk she had had as a schoolgirl, and withdrew her cheque book. Her Uncle had continued to pay an allowance into her bank and she had quite a large sum she could draw on. Then she took out a pencil and paper and wrote a brief note to Paul.

'I am going away to think things over. Please don't try to find me or bring me back because I won't come. I'm sorry for what I did . . . but I can't go on like this . . . at least I

324

don't feel I can at the moment. I will write and tell you my address as soon as I have one. You can tell Uncle and anyone else who asks I'm going for a holiday. Mary.'

She was buoyed up by her own unexpected behaviour. The lethargy that had engulfed her was gone and mentally her mind was flying in all directions, thinking, planning. She had never been away from home alone . . . and she had no idea what she would do. But the mere fact of going stimulated her into an excitement that was as unusual as it was dangerous.

She walked slowly, a trifle weakly, to the bus stop and took a bus to the station. To her relief, a train was leaving for London in ten minutes. She bought a ticket and hung back behind an advertisement board until the train came in and she could climb into an empty compartment. Once there she relaxed, suddenly tired but not yet dispirited. No one had seen her that she knew since she left the house. Paul would not know where to find her since she did not know herself where she was going.

Opposite her, a coloured print advertised the charms of Torquay. Mary thought idly that the town looked very pretty and then suddenly sat upright. Why should she not go to Torquay? It was a big town . . . large enough to lose herself there as well as she would have done in London.

Still keyed up and buoyed by the feeling of daring and adventure, Mary arrived in London, changed stations and caught a train to Torquay. Only then did she begin to feel tired and the first signs of depression took hold of her.

An elderly lady sitting beside her noticed her extreme pallor and asked if she was feeling all right.

Mary forced a smile to her lips.

'I only came out of hospital this morning . . . but I'm not ill,' she replied.

'Have you far to go?'

'Torquay,' Mary told her. 'I must find

an hotel there and then I can rest and get well again.'

'Oh, but, my dear, have you no one to look after you?' the old lady asked anxiously. 'You look to me as if you need a little cosseting. I'm sure hotel life is not the best thing.'

'I . . . I'm quite alone!' Mary said, a tremble in her voice. 'But I wish it to be like that . . . please don't worry about me.'

Seeing that the girl was near to tears, the old lady forbore to ask the questions that were on her lips. Her young companion wore a wedding ring . . . yet she did not look old enough to be married. Had she been in some kind of trouble? Was she a widow?

'I know Torquay very well!' she said at last. 'Would you be advised by me, dear, and go to a more homely place than an hotel? I can give you the address of a very nice boarding house. It is run by a dear kind lady and she would look after you until you were quite well.'

'That's very kind of you!' Mary said. 'I'd like the address.'

For the remainder of the journey, the old lady chatted away with that rather charming openness that is common to the very old and the very young. Mary was glad of the escape from her own dubious thoughts. She learned that the old lady's name was Mrs. Longman, that she lived in a tiny flat on the sea-front with her pekinese, Daybreak (because he was the child of Dawn!), that she had been visiting her married son in London, that she was seventy years old next birthday.

'I have a grandchild about your age!' she said proudly. 'A boy of twenty-seven. A young rascal, he is!'

She talked proudly of her dear Harry until at last the train drew into the station at Torquay.

Despite her age, it was Mrs. Longman who helped Mary into a taxi and went with her to the boarding house and saw her settled in. Mary was feeling so tired and ill that she knew she could not have managed alone. Within ten minutes of their arrival, her new landlady had her tucked in bed with a hot water bottle and was busy brewing her a 'nice hot cup of tea'! Kind Mrs. Longman had departed in the taxi to her own flat with a promise to call round tomorrow to see how Mary was.

Utterly exhausted, she lay back on the pillows and tried not to cry. She seemed always to be dissolving into tears now . . . and supposed that they must be the result of the miscarriage. Since everyone was being so kind to her, there was really no reason to cry . . . no reason at all, except that she wanted Paul! If he had walked into the room at this moment she knew she would have flung herself into his arms and never never let him go again.

But in the morning, she was ashamed of what she believed to have been a momentary weakness. She felt strong and refreshed by twelve hours' sleep and the sea breezes blowing in through her open window must have given her an appetite. She waded through a big breakfast which her landlady, Mrs. Pope, brought to her room.

'Will you be staying long, dear?' she asked Mary as she watched her eat.

'I . . . I don't know!' Mary said slowly. 'I . . . I haven't been very well . . . and I want to get quite fit before I . . . before I decide what to do.'

As Mrs. Longman had done, Mrs. Pope wondered what had happened to the girl. Always highly imaginative, it did cross her mind that Mary might have come out of prison! She looked so terribly white! But then she didn't look at all wicked, she told herself. On the contrary, with that cloud of fair hair spread round her shoulders and those enormous dark eyes, she looked more like an Angel from one of those oil paintings she had seen on a wet Sunday afternoon in the Art Gallery!

Well, maybe the girl would tell her in due course. She was too nice-natured to question her now. She gave her the routine for meal-times, mentioned the other guests' names, and left Mary alone to wash and dress.

At ten o'clock, as Mary completed her toilet, Mrs. Pope knocked on her door to tell her that Mrs. Longman was waiting in a taxi outside and wanted her to go home to her flat for coffee.

Having nothing else to do and wanting to thank the old lady for her kindness the night before, Mary hurried downstairs, delighted to see her new friend.

In Mrs. Longman's flat, Mary was introduced to Daybreak and had in her pleasure over the little dog's antics momentarily forgotten her reason for being in Torquay. Mrs. Longman chose this moment to say:

'I think you are in some kind of trouble, child. Won't you tell me about it?'

Mary felt the colour flare into her face as she looked up from the little dog in her arms. Mrs. Longman was sitting in front of a cosy little log fire knitting furiously, her face purposefully averted.

'I . . . I . . . I just lost my baby!' Mary felt the words dragged up from somewhere deep within her. 'It was my own fault . . . I . . . I didn't take care.'

And she burst into tears.

The relief of telling someone . . . a stranger, yet such an understanding and kindly one, was for Mary a wonderful thing. There had been no mother . . . not even Aunt Ethel . . . to whom she could let herself go and she had bottled her terrible feelings inside her too long. Now the whole story poured out into Mrs. Longman's sympathetic ears.

'But why run away from your husband?' the old lady asked when Mary ended her story. 'You still love him, don't you?'

'Yes!' Mary cried. 'No! Oh, I don't know! I am only sure that he doesn't love me any more. If he did he would be more understanding.'

Mrs. Longman forbore to say that in her view he had been very understanding . . . a lot more so than a good many young men she knew. But she had had a child of her own and she had moreover seen a grandchild through his teething troubles and knew a little of human nature. Mary was in a troubled and unhappy state of mind. Words would not put it right . . . but time might. Maybe she had done well to come away, although that poor husband of hers must be worried out of his wits.

Carefully she extracted from Mary her home address and as soon as Mary had left the flat Mrs. Longman went to her telephone. After a great deal of waiting, she at last managed to talk to Paul.

★　★　★

Paul had been frantic when he returned home to discover Mary's note. He had rushed round to her home only to find that neither Uncle Tom nor Mrs. Mayhew had seen Mary. They were as concerned as he was over her disappearance.

Paul tore home again, up to their bedroom to try and find what Mary had packed, hoping it would give him a clue to her whereabouts. But he could not remember which of her clothes were missing. He re-read her note, and on a sudden impulse, rang up his sister, Jean. But Jean was at home and there was no reply from her flat. Paul replaced the receiver and put his hand to his head. If he telephoned home, he could not ask if they had seen Mary without betraying the fact that he, himself, did not know where she was! She had said she would let him know her address! Could he just sit back and wait for her to write and tell him?

It was not in Paul's nature to sit and do nothing. He got back into his car and rushed round to Dr. Law, pouring out the whole story.

'I don't know what to suggest!' his partner said. 'She was in no fit state for a long journey. Frankly, Paul, I'm a bit worried. She took it all rather badly, I'm afraid. I wish — '

He broke off, feeling awkward in the dual relationship of being Mary's medical practitioner and Paul's friend.

'Wish what?' Paul asked bluntly. 'Look here, Dr. Law ... I know you can't tell me anything Mary said in confidence ... but did she tell you where she was going?'

The older man shook his head.

'Not even that she was going. The truth is, Paul, she would tell me nothing. I suppose she thought I'd tell you. I imagined you knew what was going on and were dealing with that side of things yourself.'

Paul sighed.

'I suppose I've made a terrible mess of things!' he said wearily. 'You know, of course, that I asked Mary to stop pushing Jackie around in that pram? You agreed with me, didn't you?'

'Most certainly! I'd have told her myself if I hadn't known you were going to put a stop to it.'

'Yes! But my telling her only made her the more determined to carry on.

She has some kind of phobia about taking my advice when it comes to Jackie. Believe me, I've done everything I could to make the child welcome . . . played with him, talked to him, made a friend of him. And I'm fond of the boy . . . and he is of me. I've never given Mary the slightest cause to think I didn't want him around or that he was anything but welcome. Why should she mistrust my motives?'

Dr. Law shook his head.

'Women can be very odd!' he said with a wry smile.

'Half the time, I don't believe they know themselves why they do these things or feel these things. Could it be that in her heart Mary knows that she wasn't playing fair by you when she accepted your offer to have Jackie live with you? It might explain why she acts on the defensive as far as he is concerned.'

'I don't see why!'

'Well, she credits you with feelings you apparently haven't had because she thinks you should be having them!'

'That sounds very involved!' Paul half laughed. 'All the same, I see what you mean. But how else could I have coped with the whole thing? I've acted only to make Mary happy. The way things have turned out, I wish I had refused to have Jackie live with us. Mary behaves quite stupidly about him ... and to risk losing her own baby ... well, I can't bear to think about it.'

'I've no doubt she is blaming herself terribly. She wanted that baby, too, Paul.'

'I know!' Paul agreed. 'That's why I'm so worried now. *Where* is she? She may be ill and alone. I must find her.'

'Short of putting the police or a private detective on the job, I don't see how you can. She did say she would write?'

Paul nodded.

'But I can't just sit back and do nothing until I hear from her. I'll go crazy!'

'Give it at least until tomorrow

337

morning,' Dr. Law said. 'We may have heard something by then. If she's really ill, we shall certainly hear something. If not, then you have no need to worry too much!'

Nonetheless, Paul spent a sleepless night. He found himself listening in the darkness to the possible ring of the telephone, the sound of Mary's key in the latch. He felt utterly wretched and filled with misgivings. Why had Mary gone? Had she stopped loving him? Was she trying to frighten him? Had she ever *really* loved him?

His thoughts swam round in circles and at last he rose and dressed and went for a walk. But once in the streets, he was afraid the phone might ring in spite of the hour of the night, and he returned home to bed to fall at last into an uneasy sleep.

He was nearly desperate when Dr. Law called him from the surgery next morning to answer the phone.

'A Mrs. Longman, from Torquay!' Dr. Law informed him as he handed over the receiver.

Paul's heart leapt and he all but shouted down the receiver:

'This is Dr. Paul Deal speaking.'

'Oh, good morning, Dr. Deal. My name is Mrs. Alice Longman. I'm ringing you from my flat in Torquay to let you know about your wife!'

'How is she? Is she there? Can I speak to her?'

'My dear young man, I cannot answer all those questions at once. Mary is not here at the moment so she cannot speak to you. Nor do I think she would if she could. May I tell you the story from the beginning?'

'Please!' Paul said, and added: 'It's very kind of you to get in touch with me. I've been frantic with worry.'

Mrs. Longman took her time telling Paul how she had met Mary on the train and the three-minute pips on the trunk line went four times before she had brought him up to date.

'She left me a few minutes ago!' Mrs. Longman finished in her thin, clear voice. 'I expect you are feeling a little piqued that she should have told a perfectly strange old lady all her feelings when she has not told you!'

'Well . . . ' Paul acknowledged the fact that he had, amongst feelings of relief and anxiety and bewilderment, been a little angry, too.

'Don't be upset! It is sometimes very much easier to pour out your heart to someone you don't know . . . and who knows only your side as you choose to relate it! I'm old enough and wise enough to see that there undoubtedly is another side . . . yours. That's why I rang you. I know from what Mary told me that you . . . you are very attached to your wife.'

'I love her very very dearly!' Paul said, uncaring of who might be listening to his sentiments. He felt an instinctive liking for and trust in this old lady although he had never met her.

'Then my advice to you, young man, is to stay just where you are and do nothing at all. Don't take the next train here.'

'But that's just what I was thinking of doing!' Paul said surprised.

'Well, don't! Don't write or let her know you know where she is. I think she needs time . . . time to get over the shock of losing her baby . . . time to lose her feeling of guilt . . . time to think clearly . . . and time to find out what love really is.'

'I . . . I don't altogether understand!' Paul said slowly.

'I could be wrong . . . but I don't think so. Your Mary is very young in some ways . . . she isn't adult in her emotions. The very fact that she has run away shows her childish frame of mind. But she is *beginning* to grow up and it is rather a painful process for her. She does love you . . . I'm sure of that. But I believe she needs to be made to realize just how much you matter to her.'

'But if I can see her . . . talk to her . . . tell her . . . '

'No! Let her be a little uncertain about *you*. She has always had your love, hasn't she? Well, let her see what life can be without it for a little while.'

'But suppose she . . . she doesn't find out? Suppose she finds she prefers being away from me? Suppose she needs me?'

'I'm sure she is beginning to need you already. As to the other questions, you being here can't force her to feel any more or less than she does. Trust her, Dr. Deal, and trust me. I'm quite certain that she loves you . . . but give her time.'

After he had extracted a promise from Mrs. Longman to ring him at least every other evening with news of Mary, and most of all her health, Paul said good-bye, and sat back in his chair, stunned by the unexpectedness of the conversation. Could this old lady be right? Had he rushed Mary too quickly into a marriage for which she was not really ready? It could make sense, and yet they had been so happy at first . . . the honeymoon . . .

Paul sighed deeply. Of course they had been happy on their honeymoon.

They had had the wonderful joy of discovering each other and the physical side of their love. It was only when they got home and the first tests came that somehow, somewhere, they had gone wrong.

He longed with all his heart to go to Mary. She was alone and unhappy and still very weak if not actually ill. His place was beside her. Yet was it not well worth sacrificing his wish to be with her if ultimately they could be together again in a new, deeper and much more lasting love?

Mary's promised letter arrived the next morning. It was curt and gave him no information he did not know already.

'*Dear Paul*,' she had written (not darling or dearest!) '*I am living at the above address. Please do not come to see me or ring me up. I want to be quite alone to think everything out. I am sorry if you have been worried about me but I had to go. I will write again when I have decided what to do.*

Mary.

P.S. I do not need any money so please don't send any.'

The postscript hurt him but he refrained from wiring her a credit to the branch of his bank in Torquay. He could let Mrs. Longman tell him if she were in need.

Her letter did not exactly sound as if she were still in love with him! He read and re-read it and puzzled over the words: *'when I have decided what to do'*. What could she do? She was his wife. Surely she could not be contemplating divorce?

To take his mind off her for a while, he sat down and wrote to his family, telling them that Mary was recuperating in Torquay if they cared to write to her there.

17

Mary sat curled up on the white fur rug in front of Mrs. Longman's fire. The old lady sat in her chair placidly knitting and listening, an enigmatic smile on her face.

'Of course, I realize it couldn't be easy for Paul having to make allowances all the time for a child who wasn't his! But don't you see, Mrs. Longman, he offered in the first place to have Jackie.'

'Maybe he thought you wouldn't marry him unless he did!'

Mary shook her head so that her hair swung on her shoulders and gleamed in the firelight.

'No! He made out to me that he would *like* Jackie to come. Then he started to object whenever my little cousin happened to be in the way. Fundamentally I think Paul has been selfish . . . yes, I do! He wanted me, but once he had what he wanted, then he was annoyed every time he had to share my responsibility.'

'Is the little boy your responsibility?' Mrs. Longman asked quietly.

'Well, of course!' Mary said indignantly. 'I always loved and cared for him and when my Aunt died, I couldn't just walk out and leave him.'

'He had his father . . . and the Mrs. Mayhew you told me about.'

'Yes, but that isn't the same as someone he knew and loved and trusted. He cries terribly whenever I leave him. You cannot expect Mrs. Mayhew to treat him like her own child.'

'Well, if Jackie's welfare is so important to you, why did you marry your Paul?'

Mary looked up surprised.

'Because I was in love with him, of course! And because he loved me . . . or I thought so.'

'But surely your Paul would want his new young wife to himself?'

'There you are!' Mary exclaimed. 'I told you he was selfish! Look at all the men who marry widows with young children . . . even grown-up families. Paul *knew* I wanted Jackie to live with us.'

'Perhaps he didn't quite realize how it was going to turn out!' Mrs. Longman said astutely.

Mary looked up at her, her face tilted sideways. There was a faint expression of uneasiness in her eyes which did not escape the old lady's gaze.

'What do you mean?'

'Only what I said. Maybe your young husband didn't foresee quite how important the child was to you . . . how much his own life was going to be affected by him.'

'You mean . . . the baby . . . our baby?'

Mrs. Longman remained silent.

Mary said suddenly:

'Well, he shouldn't have made me have a baby so soon. I told him I didn't want one yet.'

'So you took the way you did to get rid of it?'

'Oh, no!' Mary cried aghast. 'I wanted it myself . . . after a little while. I swear to you I did. I never meant to lose it. I loved my baby.' Tears threatened her but she gulped them down. 'It was Paul's fault I lost it. I might have stopped pushing Jackie around if he hadn't been so beastly!'

'Oh, my dear!' Mrs. Longman exclaimed at this childishness. 'How young you are!'

Mary had the grace to blush. But she still argued.

'You don't understand. He wasn't thinking so much of the baby when he told me to put Jackie's pram away. He said it was better for Jackie anyway. He thinks I spoil Jackie and that he's been kept more of a baby than he need be. He thinks he should go to one of those special schools for backward children.'

'Well, why not? Your husband is a doctor. He should know!'

'But Aunt Ethel would never have consented to Jackie going to school. Dr. Law suggested it once but she was right against the idea. Jackie has these fits and he couldn't be away from home.'

'There are surely trained nurses at these schools to care for children when they aren't too well?'

'I suppose so,' Mary admitted. 'All the same, I can clearly remember my Aunt telling Uncle Tom that Jackie should never go . . . that she wasn't going to allow his brain to be over-taxed or to risk his health. He might catch any childish complaints there.'

'But all children risk those complaints at school. It can't be right to keep a child back from normal activities just because you are *afraid* for it.'

Mary was quiet. She had never considered the question in quite this light. Aunt Ethel had always been afraid for Jackie. But afraid of what? Chicken-pox or measles didn't kill a child, and anyway Jackie was physically very strong indeed.

'I don't know!' she said at last. 'I . . . I suppose he could go. But why? I've always taught him his lessons myself.'

There are other things besides lessons children learn at school . . . independence, good behaviour, discipline, mixing with other children.'

'Oh, but you forget that Jackie isn't normal!'

'No! I remember it. But I think you are perhaps trying to make him a little more abnormal than he is. There are after all thousands of children, handicapped as he is or worse than he is, who go to these schools. They do wonderfully well. Besides, Mary, quite apart from Jackie's point of view, what about your own? It would leave you freer to run your home the way your husband likes it . . . to go away with him when he wants.'

Mary frowned.

'But why should I do everything just

because it pleases Paul?'

'Don't you want to please him?'

'Well, yes!' Mary said. 'But not if it conflicts with what is best for Jackie.'

Mrs. Longman put down her knitting and said matter-of-factly:

'You know, I think you made a big mistake, Mary, marrying your doctor. You don't really love him . . . not to the exclusion of all else. I think you were right to leave him. You certainly won't have been making him or yourself very happy. I think it is a good idea for you to separate and go your own ways!'

So far Mary had only poured out real and imaginary grievances. She had by no means reached the conclusion that her separation from Paul was to be a permanent arrangement. In fact she had even been considering when she might go home. Mrs. Longman's suggestion surprised her . . . and worried her, too.

'But . . . but what should I do?'

'Well, you could go home to your Uncle and look after Jackie as you think he should be looked after. It sounds to me a full-time job!'

Mary missed the faint but kindly sarcasm. She considered Mrs. Longman's remark on its own merits. Did she *want* to leave Paul . . . her husband . . . the man she was so much in love with? She did love him . . . it wasn't true what Mrs. Longman said that she did not love Paul. Was it true that she hadn't been happy living with him . . . or he with her? Certainly these last weeks had been anything but happy . . . and there had been those awful quarrels about Jackie. All the same, life without Paul was unthinkable.

She said so to her new friend.

'Oh, that's just because there is no one else!' Mrs. Longman said airily. 'Some other young man will come along and you'll stop thinking about your Paul. You just want to go back to him because there is no one better, more understanding, more willing to give way to your views.'

'But there isn't anyone I'd rather be

married to than Paul!' Mary cried. 'If I weren't married to him, I wouldn't want to be married at all. Besides, I don't believe in divorce. It surprises me that you should. I always believed your generation thought it wrong, too.'

'Oh, I don't know. Why should two people live the whole of their lives in misery when the law is willing to separate them and give them another chance?'

'Well, you make vows in church, for one thing,' Mary said stiffly. 'I happened to take mine seriously. I promised to be Paul's wife in good *and* bad times.'

'Of course, if you consider it your duty, you must go back to him.'

'I suppose I should!' Mary agreed.

'If he wants you to go back!' Mrs. Longman said casually. 'Maybe as he is so selfish a young man, he won't want the boy back, too. Then what will you do?'

Mary had not seen the trap that had been laid for her and now she was too disturbed by Mrs. Longman's remark about Paul wanting her back, to consider Jackie. Suppose Paul didn't want her back? Suppose Paul had stopped loving her? Suppose he held other views about divorce?

'Paul loves me!' she said, almost defiantly.

'But not enough to have Jackie?' Mrs. Longman asked innocently.

Mary's lips tightened.

'That's why I have come away . . . to find out!' she said. 'Paul can see how he likes living without me. I told him that if he wouldn't have Jackie, I'd go back to my Uncle. So he knows where he stands. I've sent him my address and when he's made up his mind, he can write and tell me, or come to fetch me home.'

Mrs. Longman let out her breath, smiling inwardly.

'I see! Well, that makes it all very simple. You have only to stay here quietly and wait.'

'Yes!' Mary agreed, and turned her thoughts to Daybreak who was playing with her skirt. She had never felt more unhappy or disturbed in her life.

*   *   *

Two days later, Mary's confidence had gone . . . and with it her wish to confide in Mrs. Longman, with whom she spent all her free time. She had grown very fond of the old lady, but now she had put herself in a rather difficult position. She had told her confidently that it was only a matter of time before she heard from Paul, for surely he MUST write. He could not be prepared to let her go without even a word? It was ridiculous and quite unthinkable, and it was very embarrassing to be asked two or three times a day if Paul's letter had come or if he had phoned.

'I expect he's been rather busy!' she said lamely, and went for a long walk on the sea-front that afternoon instead of going to Mrs. Longman's flat to tea.

But next morning, she was round at

the flat, waving a letter in the air, her face glowing and happy.

'From Paul?' Mrs. Longman asked with a frown, for Paul had told her on the phone last night that he hadn't written!

'No!' Mary admitted. 'It's from Jean, Paul's sister. She says they are all very sorry about the baby and she hopes I'm having a good rest in Torquay. Paul had written to ask them to write to me while I was on holiday. So you see, Paul doesn't mean this to be a permanent break.'

'No, dear, but I thought you thought he might. Then why don't you go home now?'

Mary bit her lip.

'Well, I'm still waiting to hear from Paul if he is willing for us to keep Jackie.'

'Oh, I see!'

But it wasn't just that. Paul's silence had not only surprised Mary but hurt her terribly. He had not once tele- phoned, nor replied to her note. And it was five days since she had left home!

She went out that morning and spent a brief half hour buying postcards for Paul's family. As she scribbled brief messages on the back, she felt a strong desire to write to Paul, but pride prevented her. The next move MUST come from him. She turned away from the temptation of ink and stamps and went for another long walk on the front.

There was now no question of the fact that she was better. She glowed with good health and felt physically on top of the world. But the better she felt outside, the worse she felt in her heart. Why didn't Paul write? Why didn't he phone? Could he really not want her back? Didn't he still love her after all?

She began to wonder quite how she and Paul had arrived in this position. When she had run out of the house some days ago there had been no thought of separation or divorce . . . no real desire *to leave Paul*. She had given no thought to the future or to the possible consequences of her actions.

Perhaps, she told herself wryly, I knew somewhere deep down inside me that Paul would come after me! How wrong that inner knowledge had turned out to be. Put to the test, Paul had no intention of giving way to her. He was showing by his very silence how *he* felt.

'I suppose he blames me about the baby!' she told Mrs. Longman miserably. 'He was so pleased when . . . but there would have been others. I would have had another baby!'

'Don't upset yourself, my dear!' the old lady said as she paused in her knitting to pick up a dropped stitch. 'It shouldn't be so important to you, after all . . . I mean, not if Paul has treated you so shabbily. You can't really want him back?'

But I do, I do! Mary cried in her heart.

She remained silent, her head downcast, and she did not see Mrs. Longman's soft secret smile.

That evening, when Paul telephoned

her, Mrs. Longman said:

'My methods are working beautifully, Dr. Deal. I think you might soon have a very different Mary coming home to you.'

'But when? How soon?' Paul questioned. 'You've no idea how each day drags by. If Mary knew how much I missed her . . . '

'Well, she mustn't know . . . not now. I daresay she will hate me for this deception when she discovers the truth. But that doesn't really matter very much although I have grown fond of her. Poor child . . . she needed a mother, I think, to help and advise her.'

'It seems as though you are proving a wonderful substitute!' Paul said gratefully. 'What wonderful chance it was that Mary should have got into your carriage!'

'Not chance!' Mrs. Longman corrected him. 'Providence. I believe that God takes care of His flock in His own way. Now, Dr. Deal, I intend to apply the last lesson to our little Mary. Have I your permission to act in any way I choose?'

'If it will bring her back to me!' Paul said fervently.

'Very well! Then I think I'll start tomorrow and I may have some news for you the next day.'

Mrs. Longman made another telephone call when she had said good-bye to Paul. It was to her grandson. She had a good many more than three minutes but she didn't mind that in the least. She was an old woman now and what better way to spend her money than by bringing two young people together!

'I've a lovely surprise for you, Mary!' Mrs. Longman said over coffee next morning. 'My grandson, Harry, is coming to visit me. It will be nice for you to have some young company.'

Mary flushed. She did not feel like meeting any young man, but this was Mrs. Longman's grandson whom she clearly adored and she could not refuse to meet him when Mrs. Longman had been so good and kind to her.

'We could go and meet his train together!' the old lady went on. 'Three-fifteen, he arrives! Wear something pretty, Mary. Harry is rather partial to pretty girls!'

To please Mrs. Longman, Mary made the effort. She was not in the least curious about Harry and asked no questions about him. When he stepped off the train, however, she was really surprised. Harry Longman was at least six foot two and with a wonderful physique to go with his height. He had brown hair and mischievous brown eyes and the most beautiful white teeth Mary had ever seen. Vaguely she thought of Gregory Peck and Stewart Granger and wondered how any man who was quite so handsome could still be unmarried. She stood shyly in the background while he kissed his grandmother and was astounded to see him twinkling at her over the little old lady's shoulder.

A moment later, he was kissing *her* cheek, too.

'She's just as pretty as you told me she would be!' he said to his grandmother. 'This is going to be fun!'

In the taxi driving them to the flat, Harry stared openly at Mary, and conscious of his gaze, Mary knew herself to be blushing and hopelessly confused. There was no doubt about the fact that Harry was flirting with her. Did he know she was married or didn't it make any difference to him? Mary tended rather to the latter view. Harry looked as if he had been made of mischief ... his curling mouth, his eyes, the lines of his face, all showed an amusing, humorous and slightly 'devilish' quality which she had never come across before.

He talked incessantly ... amusing light banter which made his grandmother laugh and Mary smile shyly. 'At least,' she thought, 'I can stop thinking about Paul.' Harry Longman's personality was such that it allowed no room for anyone else on the scene!

'Can we go places tonight, Gran?' he asked as they sat round the fire over their tea. 'I'd like to take Mary out.'

'Oh, I can't go out ... ' Mary began, but Mrs. Longman interrupted with a quiet:

'Oh, but of course, Mary dear. I'm relying on you to help me keep Harry amused. He has so many friends in London and when he comes here I never know what to do with him to keep him from getting bored.'

'I expect we can find somewhere, Mary, sweet Mary,' said Harry.

Mary looked distressed.

'Really, I'd rather stay and keep your grandmother company!' she said. It would be disloyal to go out and amuse herself when Paul might be worrying. *But Paul wasn't worrying.* Still he had not written or phoned ...

'Very well, I will come!' she said defiantly. 'I'd like to go out with you!'

'That's the spirit!' Harry said. 'I'll

363

call for you at seven-thirty.'

Mary's defiance lasted her until she was sitting opposite Harry at the dinner table in the restaurant he had chosen ... the best in the place! Then, as Harry paid her extravagant compliments and told her for the fifth time how pretty she was and what fun they were going to have this week of his visit, she began to feel conscience-stricken ... not only about Paul, but about Harry, too.

'Your grandmother did tell you I ... I'm married?' she said when he paused for a few moments.

Harry grinned.

'Oh, yes, Granny warned me! But all's fair in love and war, Mary. She said you'd left your husband ... that he'd been a brute to you and you were well rid of him. So I reckon that leaves you free, doesn't it?'

Mary felt herself even more confused. It was not true that she had left Paul ... at least, not in the sense Mrs. Longman inferred. Nor was it true that

Paul was a brute! Least true of all was the fact that she was free. She still felt as deeply and truly married to Paul as if her were here in the room beside her. She felt it quite wrong to be sitting here with an attractive young man, letting him flirt with her. Yet how did one stop Harry Longman flirting?

'Come now, Mary, don't spoil the evening with thoughts about the past. We're going to have a good time and forget that unpleasant husband of yours. Mary, have I told you how perfectly stunning you are? That combination of fair hair and brown eyes!'

Mary smiled and then her face grew serious again as she remembered Paul had said much the same thing. Paul . . . Paul . . .

'I insist that you listen to me when I'm flattering you so prettily!' Harry interrupted her memories. 'Come now, Mary, tell me if I stand a chance of making you fall just a little bit in love with me?'

It was impossible to take Harry

seriously and yet she felt herself to be at a loss to deal with him. From anyone else, his remarks would seem very forward, very intimate for a few hours' acquaintance, and yet from Harry they came so naturally that she could not be cross. He was in any case quite irrepressible, as she was to find out.

He discovered a dance in progress in the Town Hall and insisted they go to it.

'It'll be enormous fun after the sophistication of London night clubs. Let's go, Mary!'

In a way, it was fun . . . and Mary might have enjoyed it tremendously had it not been for the thought of Paul . . . of the last time she had danced with him . . . of the thrill of his holding her. Harry, too, was drawing her close against him, his cheek touching hers, but it didn't mean anything to her . . . only a great sense of loss that it should not be Paul.

She was too honest to close her eyes and pretend. Harry seemed not to notice her lack of response and behaved gaily and ridiculously and charmingly throughout the dance. As they left, he tucked his arm beneath hers and held her hand.

'My lovely Mary is tired!' he said. 'I'm going to take you home.'

'If only it were not for Paul!' Mary thought. 'How wonderful this could have been.' Harry was not only handsome and amusing but kind and thoughtful too. She might even have fallen in love with him if . . . always that if. Her heart was Paul's and always would be.

'Forget about that husband of yours!' Harry said as the taxi drove slowly along the sea-front. 'You've been thinking about him all evening. Kiss me, Mary!'

His lips were touching hers before she could speak her refusal. It was an answer to her loneliness, her despair, to her wounded pride, and for a brief while she allowed Harry to kiss her, even returned his kisses. If Paul did not want her, then there was someone else who did! she thought defiantly. But it did not last for long and a moment later two tears trickled down her cheek and Harry said:

'I've not made you cry, Mary?'

She shook her head, brushing the tears away angrily.

'No! It isn't you, Harry . . . it's . . . it's . . . just that life can be so difficult!'

'Perhaps you take it too seriously!' Harry said lightly. 'Divorce that husband of yours and marry me, Mary. I'll make you laugh!'

Mary smiled tremulously. Harry somehow did not fit into the category of husband. All the same, it was a comfort to know he found her attractive.

'I'll change your mind for you!' Harry grinned cheerfully. 'By the end of the week, you'll be coming back to London with me. You know, I'm already quite a bit in love with you, Mary. You're so different from . . . '

'From all your other girl-friends?' Mary teased.

Then the taxi stopped outside her

'digs' and Harry dropped a light kiss on her cheek and said 'good night!' His cheery smile stayed with her until she closed the front door and then she was again alone.

18

'Of course, she's still head over heels in love with that husband of hers!' Harry told his grandmother as he perched on the end of her bed. 'Even my charms would not make her forget him for long!'

Mrs. Longman chuckled.

'Ha! Just what I thought. Well, it's a question of time . . . that's all.'

'You're a wicked old schemer!' Harry said, smiling at the old lady. 'Always were! Still, I am a little piqued to think that for once I've failed to make much of an impression.'

'Do you the world of good!' his grandmother said bluntly. 'Far too many young women throwing themselves at your head. You're far too eligible, Harry. I'm considering disinheriting you.'

'Come off it, Gran!' Harry said

indignantly. 'It isn't my money the girls are after . . . it's me!'

'So I suspect!' Mrs. Longman said, thinking how attractive and charming this young grandson of hers was . . . how irresistible to the opposite sex. If Mary could still think of Paul with Harry around, then she must be in love!

She sighed.

'You know, I've grown so fond of Mary. I'm beginning to wish she were not married and you and she — '

'No, Gran, darling!' Harry said, for once speaking seriously. 'She's far too gentle and sweet. I'd be horribly unkind to a girl like that. I need someone who can stand up to me!'

'Wish I knew the right girl!' his grandmother said. 'I'd like to see you settled down, Harry . . . I'd like some great-grandchildren, you know!'

'I'll see if I can find her!' Harry said, kissing his grandmother good night. 'All the same, I like your little Mary.'

* * *

For the next three days, Harry 'squired' Mary round Torquay, obedient to his grandmother's suggestion that he should make himself as attentive and attractive as possible. The trouble with Mary, his grandmother had told him, was that she had married the first man she had met, or practically! Paul had been in love with her from the first moment and she had been taking his love too much for granted, beside the fact that she had not been able to place in an important enough place her own love for Paul.

'I want her to find out for herself, Harry, that NO OTHER MAN will do. If she can remain immune to your charms then it will make her realize once and for all how completely she belongs to that young husband of hers.'

'But suppose she falls in love with me?' Harry had asked. 'Devil of a mess that would be, Gran!'

'I think I know Mary won't do that!' his grandmother had said. Now Harry wondered if she had deliberately chosen those particular words in order to get him to comply to her little plan. It was enough to pique any man's pride, and especially his, since he had been 'chased' by women ever since he left school. He had never had to exert himself to get a girl-friend . . . or to make a girl care for him. Perhaps for that reason, he had never fallen in love himself except in a light-hearted way. As soon as he found the girl was falling seriously in love with him, he had realized that he had no wish or intention of settling down to 'married bliss' and had ended the affair quickly.

Mary intrigued him. As he grew to know her better, he became more deeply interested in her and consequently his manner with her changed. He could no longer be flippant . . . steal a kiss lightly . . . laugh when she had that lost sad expression in her eyes. He was uncomfortably made aware that his pretended flirtation with her had ceased to be pretence or flirtation. In spite of what he had told his grandmother he was beginning to fall in love. He told himself with unaccustomed introspection that Mary wasn't 'his type' . . . that she was much too kind and sweet to be his kind of girl . . . that anyway, she was a married woman and unquestionably in love with her husband, even if she didn't know it. What had started out as an innocent little game invented by his grandmother had somehow or other turned into a far more serious matter than he had ever believed possible.

As each day brought him closer to understanding of Mary, as he learned more about her and her life, spent longer hours in her company, he knew himself to be ensnared ever a little deeper in this net of his grandmother's making. He had begun to consider that he should return to London . . . forget all about her . . . put an end to this nonsense. But he was strangely weak and found he could not go.

Mary's behaviour towards him was partly responsible.

After that first evening dancing with

Harry ... when she had been so terribly unhappy and had allowed Harry to kiss her, she had been doing quite a bit of thinking. She knew that Harry was not of a serious nature ... that he was only amusing himself and that a kiss meant nothing to him. She did not dislike him because he was that way. Somehow it made their relationship very much simpler. Had he been of a thoughtful, serious disposition she would never have agreed to go on seeing him ... let alone spending most of her time in his company.

She puzzled a little over his grandmother's attitude to them both. That respectable old lady was doing her utmost to throw them together although she knew Mary was married! It hardly seemed in character unless she had sufficient confidence in Mary and her grandson not to suspect them of anything but a platonic friendship. Yet if that were so, she could not know Harry very well! He was hardly the type for platonic friendships. Nevertheless, she had found to her surprise as she grew to know Harry better that he was not so will-o'-the-wisp as his manner with her that first evening had led her to suppose. He had not tried to kiss her again and Mary found to her pleasure that Harry was growing to mean much what an elder brother might mean to her. He was excellent company . . . striving to amuse her and keep her from brooding over Paul's silence. Yet he could talk seriously when the occasion demanded. It never occurred to Mary that there was far more to be worried about in Harry's good behaviour than if he were casual and flirtatious. She never guessed that Harry was falling in love.

Watching them and listening to them when they sat by the fire and chattered to each other, old Mrs. Longman felt a variety of different emotions. Perhaps the strongest of all was that this could not last. In the seven or eight odd years since Harry had grown up and chased round London behaving like a dilettante, she had begun to despair that he would ever settle down and find real happiness. Harry was very very dear to her; ever since he had been a tiny boy, there had been something special in their relationship. She alone knew that beneath the casual flippancy and care-nought attitude he presented to the world, he was generous, good, even sentimental! She was the first to admit that he was spoilt . . . had always been thoroughly spoilt by the attention of the opposite sex. Few women could resist Harry's good looks, his cheerful disposition and his innate charm and good manners. If they had not thrown themselves at his head, he might have taken them more seriously . . . had a little more respect for them. As it was, she suspected he rather despised them even while they amused him at times.

But with Mary, Harry was different. At first, she had believed as Mary did in a delightful brother and sister relationship existing between them. Harry had professed himself as liking Mary very much that first evening they had met, but confessed that she wasn't his 'type' . . . that he could never marry a girl like Mary. But now Mrs. Longman wondered if Harry knew himself well enough to judge for himself. And while part of her was pleased to see Harry so obviously growing fond of a sweet, gentle girl like Mary, the greater half of her began to be a little afraid in case her plans were going wrong and Harry was falling in love.

This was the very last thing she wanted, since she had no doubt that Mary loved her husband and knew for a fact that the young Doctor Deal was deeply in love with his wife. Here again, her plans were going wrong. Was this to be a lesson to her not to meddle with other people's love affairs? She had told Paul that on no account should he come running after Mary . . . that he should wait for her to come back to him. Now she wasn't so sure. Mary was making no move to return to Paul although it was nearly three weeks since she had left him. Harry had announced his intention of staying a further week with his grandmother. Now Paul, when she advised him to come and see his wife on the telephone last night, had said:

'But surely your advice to me was to wait for Mary to come back? Of course, I could come down . . . tomorrow if necessary!'

'Well, I think maybe it might be a good idea!' Mrs. Longman said thoughtfully.

'A week ago I would have agreed whole-heartedly,' Paul replied after a moment's silence. 'Now I'm not so sure. Mary walked out on me and it's up to her to come back if she wishes.'

'That's just your pride speaking,' Mrs. Longman told him.

'All right, I'll accept that,' Paul agreed. 'But I find I do have that pride.'

'Surely it is not more important to you than your love for your wife?'

'No!' Paul agreed. 'But the more I have thought about Mary's behaviour, the more certain I have become that she doesn't love me. In a hundred years I could never have walked out on her!'

'But I am completely certain she is in love with you, Dr. Deal,' Mrs. Longman said.

'Then why doesn't she come back?' Paul retorted.

Why didn't Mary go back? Mrs. Longman debated the question anxiously. Had she herself advised her not to? No! On the other hand she had made life much pleasanter for Mary than it would have been if she'd found herself alone in Torquay. She had provided her with an amusing companion in Harry.

She found an opportunity to talk the matter over with Mary . . . not an easy thing to do since Mary was unaware of her phone calls to and from Paul.

'Paul can't love me very much since he has neither written nor made any attempt to find me!' Mary said flatly.

'Now you are letting pride get the better of your love, Mary,' Mrs. Longman said anxiously. 'You yourself told me that Paul matters more to you than anyone in the world. Yet you are too proud to go back and tell him you are sorry.'

'But I'm not sorry!' Mary said. 'If this is all Paul cares about me, then much as I love him, I don't want to go on living with him. It's better I should find it out now!'

Mrs. Longman developed a very unhappy frame of mind. No doubt about the fact that she had made a nasty mess of things this time . . . and she had so wanted to be fairy godmother to Mary and Paul . . . wave her hand and see everything coming out right for them. How was she to put things right now? Confess to Mary that she and Paul had been in constant touch about her? Yet Mary would be very angry if she knew! Confess to Paul that Mary was deeply hurt by the silence she had advocated and too proud to make the first move towards reconciliation?

She decided to talk it over with Harry

. . . but he, for once, was very unsympathetic.

'It's all very well to interfere with other people's lives, Gran. You never get thanked for it . . . and in any case, I think you ought not to have done what you did. Oh, I know your intentions were for the best . . . and maybe at first they did work out as you meant them to. But things have a way of getting out of hand when you deal with human emotions, don't they?'

'I don't see what *you're* worrying about, Harry dear.'

'No!' Harry said shortly. 'I don't suppose you do, Gran!'

His grandmother looked at him anxiously.

'Harry, you . . . you aren't falling in love with Mary?'

Harry gave a laugh which had none of its usual happiness or gaiety.

'Silly, isn't it? To let oneself get serious about a girl who loves someone else . . . is married to someone else at that!'

'Oh, Harry!' his grandmother said, and burst into tears.

Harry forgot his own private worries while he tried to reassure and comfort her.

'Don't worry, Gran darling. I'll get over it. And we'll find some way to get Mary back to Paul. Now don't cry any more, darling. You'll spoil your pretty face!'

She allowed him to coax back a smile, but she was still a very worried old lady as she pondered what to do next!

19

'You are an ass, Paul!' Jean said as she took the glass of sherry he offered her. 'Why in heaven's name didn't you tell me all this sooner?'

Paul gave a wry grin.

'Pride, I suppose! It's not very nice having to tell your family your wife has left you!'

'Oh, nonsense, Paul!' Jean said briskly. 'Of course Mary hasn't left you. And you as a doctor should understand better than most husbands how upsetting a miscarriage can be. Besides, it is ridiculous to say she never wanted the baby. You know as well as I do that whatever she may have said or thought *at first* she was looking forward terribly to having the child. It's my belief she went away because she *felt* you blamed her.'

'I never gave her a moment's reason

for thinking I did!' Paul replied with heat.

'It may have been better if you had said so!' Jean said. 'It would have cleared the air. Sometimes too much kindness can be wrong . . . make Mary feel even worse than she did . . . guiltier. I think you should have been very angry with her.'

'I was angry!' Paul admitted. 'But not to Mary. I couldn't let her see it, Jean . . . nor would you if you could have seen her lying there in bed, deathly white and . . . and broken!'

Jean sighed.

'Why are men so silly? I believe most women like their men to *be* men. Did I tell you I'd broken it off with Edwin? Oh, don't be sympathetic about it. He'll survive. And he'll be a lot happier without me. I'd have ended up making him miserable, bullying him. He's far too subservient for me!'

Paul shrugged his shoulders.

'I really don't understand you

women!' he said truthfully. 'You're trying to tell me women don't want kindness and sympathy.'

'Of course they want it . . . at the right time!' Jean said enigmatically. 'But at other times they want to be mastered and . . . and swept off their feet. Bullied, even. I think if you'd taken the first train to Torquay and torn a few strips off Mary for running out on you, then taken her in your arms, you'd have been happily discussing the start of a new baby by now!'

'But Mrs. Longman strongly advised me not to!' Paul argued.

'Stuff!' Jean said rudely. 'Some old lady with a misguided wish to be kind! How can you let her . . . a stranger . . . judge what's best for you and your wife! If I were Mary, and if I knew . . . I'd be mad as hell!'

'Oh, blast!' Paul said furiously. 'I suppose you might be right, Jean, but it's done now. How to undo it?'

'Swallow your pride and go down there!' Jean said. 'Tomorrow!'

Paul passed a hand wearily across his forehead.

'I can't, Jean. I've two cases going into hospital tomorrow morning for operations and a baby due tomorrow, too. I *can't* get away.'

'I suppose that's my cue to offer to go down as your ambassador!' Jean said with raised eyebrows. But Paul looked so wretchedly white and strained that she weakened and said:

'You write her a letter, Paul . . . tell her everything . . . every little thing you've felt . . . truthfully. Tell her you don't want Jackie back to live with you . . . that you'll have him if she makes it a condition of returning because you want her back at all costs . . . you know what I mean, Paul . . . the real truth!'

'Perhaps that's where I went wrong!' Paul agreed unhappily. 'I pretended to want Jackie because I knew *she* wanted it. Deep down inside her, I suppose she guessed. I never thought it would work out . . . and what happened eventually proved I was right!'

'Very humiliating for Mary!' Jean said caustically. 'That's one of the things I wouldn't put in the letter, Paul! You know, Mary has behaved very stupidly . . . oh, don't jump to her defence like that! She has! The only excuse for her is that she hasn't grown up . . . hadn't grown up when you married her, Paul. You shouldn't have rushed her, you know.'

'I was in love with her!' Paul said quietly. 'I suppose I was selfish but I wanted her so badly, Jean.'

'I know!' Jean said, suddenly gentle and kind. 'At least, I think I know. I've come to the conclusion I've never really been in love . . . for all my little affairs. Wonder if I ever shall meet the *right* man?'

'I hope so!' Paul said sincerely. 'He'll get a wonderful wife, Jean.'

'No!' Jean said honestly. 'I'm really very selfish at heart, Paul. My husband won't have an easy time at all!'

'Marriage isn't easy for anyone!' Paul said thoughtfully. 'How can it be, Jean, when you consider it. Two children grow up in different worlds with different parents and outlook and schooling and tastes and interests. Then they meet and fall in love and suddenly they have to live as one person. I would never have believed that Mary and I could quarrel. I love Mary . . . I'd do anything in the world for her . . . even have the boy back. I know that now.'

'Then don't let her know it!' Jean said. 'I think that is one of the reasons marriages go wrong sometimes . . . too much giving. It seems a queer thing to say . . . but that is one of the reasons I've ended my engagement to Edwin. He tried to merge his personality into mine . . . to give way to everything I ever wanted because he loved me too much. He wanted to be just what I wanted, instead of himself. People should retain their individuality . . . respect each other's individuality as separate people. After all, if you change the person they fell in love with into someone else, then they cease to be the person you wanted as a partner!'

'That's horribly profound!' Paul said. 'And I don't altogether agree. Retain your individuality by all means, but one of the great joys of loving someone is the pleasure it gives you to give to them.'

'I've never felt that for anyone!' Jean admitted. 'Maybe I'm not capable of a selfless love.'

'Of course you are!' Paul laughed. 'It'll hit you when you least expect it, Jean. Just wait and see!'

* * *

It was a brilliant starry night and Harry, to his surprise, found himself enjoying the late night walk along the sea-front. Walking had never been one of his pleasures till now ... yet he could understand why it seemed so marvellous tonight ... it was because Mary was with him.

'Mary, what are you going to do?' he asked suddenly. 'About the future, I mean?'

Mary bit her lip.

'I don't know, Harry. I still love Paul . . . I suppose I always will . . . but I'll never go back now . . . it's too late!'

'Why?'

'Don't you see, I can't go back to living my life with a man who doesn't love me!' Mary cried wretchedly. 'Whatever I did to Paul . . . however much I hurt him . . . he could surely have found it in his heart to forgive me . . . if he loved me.'

It was on the tip of Harry's tongue to tell Mary the truth . . . that Paul had never ceased to worry about her and had been in constant touch with his grandmother from the first day he knew of her whereabouts.

'Are you absolutely sure you love him?' he asked. 'Surely if you did, Mary, you'd go back?'

'No!' she said. 'I can't go back. I can't.'

'Even if you were certain he still loved you?'

Mary shook her head in a little

gesture of torment.

'Harry, don't let's talk about love. You told me yourself you had never been in love. You can't understand how . . . how deep and terrible a thing it can be!'

'Can't I?' Harry asked bitterly. 'A week ago I'd have agreed with you, Mary. Not now! You see, I do know what it means to be in love. I love you. I love you with a feeling that no mere words can express. Oh, don't turn away from me like that. Let me say it, Mary. I never meant to do so, but now I must tell you. If you were only free I'd ask you to marry me. If I thought you were free of your love for Paul, I'd beg you to come away with me now . . . to leave him and start a new life. I love you, Mary. I want to take care of you and protect you. Most of all I want your happiness!'

Mary was so astounded by Harry's words that her surprise overcame her natural caution.

'Do you really mean all that, Harry?' He was suddenly hurt and a little angry, too. He stopped her abruptly and without warning put his arms round her and kissed her full on the lips . . . a long kiss . . . a kiss he had wanted to give for days.

'That will show you I mean it!' he said as she drew away from him. Instantly, he regretted his action, for Mary was in tears. She cried silently, the tears slipping down her cheeks.

'Oh, don't, please don't!' Harry said wretchedly. 'Forget I did it, Mary. Darling, I'm sorry!'

He guided her to a bench where they both sat down. Mary fought for control and at last said in a choked little voice:

'It isn't for you to be sorry, Harry. It's I! Wherever I go I seem to make a mess of everything. I never guessed you were *serious*, Harry.'

'Nor did I!' Harry spoke in strained tones. 'And nor, I think, does my fond grandmother. It's really all her fault, Mary, if anyone is to blame. I suppose I'd better tell you the whole story. You'll probably be very angry when you hear it. But I think this has gone on long enough . . . for all of us.'

'Tell me what?' Mary asked, her face white in the starlight. 'What is it, Harry?'

As briefly as he could, he told her.

'Try not to blame Gran!' he said at last. 'She wanted your happiness, Mary, and Paul's. I was just a pawn in the game . . . someone she thought of who could make you see just how much you did love your husband. She took a chance, of course, in risking the fact that you might fall in love with me! But there wasn't ever any risk, was there, Mary? Heart and soul you belong to Paul!'

Mary was trembling. She felt most of all the emotions that assailed her, bitterly ashamed. She had been no more than a puppet on a stage. Everyone else knew what was going on except herself! It was cruel of them . . . cruel . . . and humiliating. She had been taught a lesson. A lesson she needed to learn? she asked herself bitterly. Even if it were so, how could Paul have subjected her to this?

She must have spoken her last thoughts aloud, for Harry said:

'Don't blame your husband, Mary! He wanted to come down on the next train to fetch you. It was my grandmother who insisted he should not do so. She meant it for the best, Mary. You see, she believed you loved Paul but that you'd never really had a chance to find out just what he did mean to you. That's why she asked me to come down and take you out and flirt with you a bit. She said you'd never had the chance most girls get of comparing Paul to other men they'd known. It was really to help you get to know yourself!'

'I see!' Mary said bitterly. 'So you've been lying to me, too?'

'No!' Harry said. 'At least don't doubt me, Mary. When I first met you, I told Gran you weren't my type . . . that you were far too good and sweet and kind for me . . . but it didn't work out that way. Despite everything,

I fell in love with you.'

'Does she know?' Mary asked.

Harry shook his head.

'I didn't mean to tell even you!' he said. 'I was going back to London tomorrow . . . to try and forget you. That's why I asked you tonight what you meant to do about the future. You see, I still had just a very faint hope that you might not want to return to your husband. I'd no grounds for that hope except that I wanted to believe it existed.'

Mary could not find words to express all that was in her heart. She had never felt so hopelessly confused or so torn by emotions that replaced one another with frightening speed. Paul had *wanted* to come . . . yet he had let someone prevent him! He still loved her . . . yet he thought she needed to be taught to love him! And Harry . . . dear Harry . . . he only imagined himself in love with her. Somehow she was sure at least of that. She could see that her very disinterest in him might have led him to find a greater interest in her! And his grandmother . . . the woman she had believed her friend . . . how could she have kept Paul from her? Now she could never trust Paul again!

'I suppose . . . there is no hope . . . for me?' Harry asked. 'You don't love me at all, do you, Mary?'

'But I do!' Mary cried. 'Not the way *you* mean, Harry, but as a friend . . . as a kind of brother. You've been so wonderful to me and I'll always, always be grateful.' She turned her attention fully to the unhappy boy beside her. 'Harry,' she said gently with new-found wisdom . . . 'You said yourself that I was not 'your type'. I believe that's true. Deep in your heart, you know it is true, too. You just think you're in love with me because you've felt sorry for me and because we're such good companions. But having a good time together doesn't mean we'd suit one another. Love . . . real love . . . is something quite else. It's knowing that nothing else in the whole world matters if you can't be with that person . . . that life is empty and meaningless if they don't love you . . . that there could never, never be anyone else.'

'The way you feel about Paul?'

'Yes!' Mary said simply. 'The way I feel about Paul. I can see now that I've only just learned the meaning of love. I've found out what it was like living without Paul . . . thinking he did not care. I've found out that after all pride doesn't matter either. I'll go back to Paul and tell him I'm sorry . . . sorry for being so selfish and unreasonable. I wanted Paul but I wasn't prepared to sacrifice anything for him . . . that's why I jumped at his offer to have Jackie. This time, I'm going to live my life the way Paul wants it.'

'He's a damned lucky fellow!' Harry said enviously. 'Oh, Mary, I can't bear to think I might not see you any more!'

'Must we stop seeing each other?' Mary asked simply. 'Couldn't you stop thinking yourself in love so that we can go on being good friends?'

'I suppose I could try!' Harry grinned. 'Maybe if I see you with that paragon of all virtues, your husband, I shall begin to feel you're a married woman . . . happily married at that.'

'Maybe he won't want me back!' Mary said, suddenly cold as she considered the fact.

Harry laughed.

'No fear of that, Mary. I'm afraid he loves you all right. Gran has no doubts about that!'

'Your grandmother!' Mary said crossly, and then broke off laughing. 'Well, maybe she was right . . . maybe I needed this to make me see things straight. I'll try not to be too cross with her, Harry.'

'Sleep on it!' Harry advised. 'When you come round to the flat in the morning, you'll be calmer. Poor old Gran!'

Mary was calm when she took a taxi to Mrs. Longman's flat the next morning. She had packed her suitcases and paid her bill and was ready for her journey home. She had slept little that night, her whole being torn with this newly-discovered love for Paul. She could not understand now how she could ever have left him! Far less let her pride stop her from returning to him. She longed to lift the telephone and hear his voice and yet she wanted more even than that to see the expression on his face when he opened his front door that evening and found her there, in their home!

She was tortured now by her longing to be with him . . . to see for herself from his eyes that he did truly love her and want her home

Harry opened the door to her and drew her into the hall.

'Someone here . . . to surprise you!' he whispered.

Mary gasped.

'Not . . . not Paul?'

He shook his head.

'No! His sister, Jean. She was just coming round to your digs.'

A moment later, Mary and Jean were embracing warmly, Mrs. Longman and Harry watching them with mixed feelings.

'You silly goose, Mary!' Jean was saying. 'I've a letter here, from Paul, telling you to come home right away. He wanted to come himself but he really couldn't get away from his work . . . and that's the absolute truth. I'll guarantee it.'

'I . . . I was going back anyway . . . today!' Mary said in a voice so choked with happiness that it sounded as if she might cry.

'She's obviously dying to read that letter!' Mrs. Longman said. 'Go into the kitchen, Mary, and read it in peace!'

'So that's that!' Harry said, offering Jean a cigarette, and as he held up his lighter, meeting her dark eyes across the flame, suddenly his spirits lightened. He even found himself grinning a little when he had expected to be drowning his sorrows. What was it that caused this sudden lightening of his spirits?

This girl, with her rather mischievous dark eyes? Mary's husband's sister! Was she like him to look at? If so, he could understand why Mary found Paul attractive. This girl certainly had 'something'. She was very smartly dressed, casually but with that chic which Harry liked in a woman.

He took his eyes away from the long white fingers which he had just noted were ringless and listened to what she was saying about trains back to London.

'Well, I'm going up myself on the four-fifteen!' he said eagerly. 'What about lunching with Gran and myself and coming up with me?'

'I'd love to!' Jean said. She turned to the old lady. 'You know, I think you have been very naughty to keep your grandson a secret from Paul. I'm quite sure if he knew this was the kind of friend Mary had in Torquay he'd have been down by jet plane!'

'Well, I did tell your brother I had my grandson here!' Mrs. Longman said, smiling.

Jean grimaced.

'He thought you meant a small boy!' she said.

'That's all Harry is at heart, bless him!' Mrs. Longman said. 'He's just a little bit in love with Mary, Miss Deal. You'll have to try and mend his broken heart!'

For a moment, Harry was disconcerted. Could his grandmother have any idea of the feelings he had expressed to Mary last night? But how could she! He even wondered a little how he had let himself go the way he had. Of course, he was fond of Mary . . . a little in love with her . . . but maybe it wouldn't have worked out after all. If he were really deeply in love, he surely couldn't find himself thinking her sister-in-law so attractive!

'As a matter of fact, I've just broken my engagement!' Jean said, smiling. 'So I could do with a little cheering up, too.'

'Really?' Harry asked eagerly. 'Then we're both more or less in the same boat. What about a dinner-dance in London this evening? Could you make it?'

'Not tonight!' Jean said. 'But another night I'd love it.'

So there were other men-friends to take her out and give her a good time! Harry thought as Jean had wished him to think. 'Well, tomorrow then?' he asked and she told him she'd give him her phone number so he could ring her.

Mrs. Longman smiled a little secret smile. It looked as if Harry had met his match at last. And what a pretty girl Jean was! Modern, yes, but in a nice way. Looking at the two of them standing there beside each other, she could feel somewhere deep down inside her that they were 'right' together. What a handsome couple they made!

But this time she would not meddle. She had learnt her lesson. She knew from Harry how angry Mary was and was just a little afraid of what the girl would say before she went home to her nice young husband.

When Mary returned from the kitchen, however, she was too starry-eyed and happy to be angry with anyone.

'Dear Mrs. Longman,' she said as she took the old lady's hand. 'You've been so kind . . . and . . . and wise!'

For she was glad now that it had all worked out as it had done . . . that she had decided to go home of her own accord . . . to be the one to cast aside her useless pride. Now Paul had done the same . . . his letter telling her again and again how much he loved her, needed her, wanted her home again.

There was still Jackie . . . Paul had told her exactly how he felt about the boy.

' . . . I want you all to myself, darling, but not if it will make you unhappy. Somehow I feel in my heart that you worry too much about the child. Believe me, dearest, he is not so dependent on you as you believe. He has settled down since you left with Mrs. Mayhew and his father and

405

Uncle Tom tells me he wants Jackie to go to school if they'll take him. Darling, if Jackie means more to you than anything in the world, how can you have left him these last three weeks when you wouldn't leave him for a week-end when I wanted to take you home? Can't you see, my dearest, that you only feel you ought to want him, but that deep in your heart, while you love him dearly, you don't need him any more than he needs you. It is because I know this that I risk telling you how I feel. I want us to be together, Mary, alone . . . with our own family . . . with nothing between us. Can it not be so? If I am wrong and you do want and need the child, then he shall come back to live with us and we will never speak of this again. I want only your happiness, Mary . . . '

She knew now that Paul was right. She could not reconcile her refusal to part from Jackie for a week-end with her own desertion of him for three weeks! And if Paul said that Jackie had settled down happily with Mrs. Mayhew, maybe he did not need her after all. Maybe she had only wished him to need her because she clung to her old life when she began her new life with Paul. If Jackie stayed with his father, then she and Paul could start again with nothing between them . . . no past . . . only the present and the future.

'You'll have to hurry if you're catching the two-ten!' Harry said. 'Jean and I will come and see you off!'

As Mary looked out of the train window and waved to their receding figures, she too was struck as Mrs. Longman had been by the 'rightness' of them . . . both so tall and good-looking. Maybe this was the answer to Harry . . . he and Jean! The thought made her very happy for next to Paul they were the two dearest friends she had.

'I must tell Paul!' she thought, and forgot everything but the fact that at last she was going home to him.

20

She was tired but wonderfully happy when she slipped the key in the lock of her own little house. It was quite dark. As she switched on the hall light she saw a note propped up on the table.

'Supper's in the oven, sir. Mrs. Ewin wants you to call her.

Bessie.'

The smile faded from her eyes as she realized fully for the first time what she had done. She had walked out on her own husband, leaving him without thought to Bessie's cares ... to warmed-up meals in the oven, phone messages and no welcome home. How could she have done it? But it would be different tonight.

She hurried upstairs after making sure the sitting-room fire was alight, and quickly bathed and changed into a blue wool frock . . . one Paul had admired on their honeymoon. It took her a little time to comb her fair hair into the style she wished, to make up her face. Then she was downstairs again, hurriedly placing the little oak table in front of the now blazing fire and laying two places with candlesticks between them.

In the kitchen she found that Bessie had left a pie but nothing else, so she raided her own store cupboard to produce some tinned grapefruit, and was busy making a caramel custard when she heard Paul's key in the lock. She paused in her work, standing perfectly still, her heart turning over and over inside her. He would, of course, realize someone was home since she had left on several lights. A second later she heard his voice:

'Bessie? You still here?'

Then as his footsteps came towards her, she turned and ran to the door. The next instant, she was gathered close against his heart.

'Mary, you, *you*?' he was saying as if he could not believe his own eyes. 'Oh, darling, darling, I never imagined you could be home so soon . . . Jean only left this morning and I worked out that at the soonest you would come tomorrow. Mary, is it really you?'

'Oh, Paul!' she half laughed, half cried as she clung to him. 'I was coming anyway. I'd called in to bid Mrs. Longman and Harry good-bye and found Jean there with your letter. But I was coming anyway.'

The look on his face could only be described as transfigured as he took in the import of her words. A moment later, his lips were on hers and there was no need then for explanations. Nothing in the whole world mattered to either of them but this.

Later, the words poured from both of them. The meal untouched, they sat arms entwined close against each other on the sofa. Paul was saying:

'We'll have another honeymoon,

dearest, as soon as I can get away from work.'

'No, darling!' Mary said, shaking her head. 'I've come home to be your wife, Paul . . . not just . . . ' she smiled shyly, 'not just your lover. I mean to be a real wife this time. I want us to be here together, darling, so that I can prove to you I can be the kind of girl you want to live your life with.'

'As if there could ever be any other!' Paul said, touching the palm of her hand with little kisses. 'Oh, Mary, I've missed you so terribly. It has been horrible without you.' Then, because he was afraid she might think he was reproaching her, he said: 'I know I could have put an end to our separation sooner but I felt I had no right to hurry you a second time. I rushed you into marriage in a way, didn't I? Before you were really ready for it.'

'No!' Mary replied honestly. 'I was ready for it, Paul, but I wasn't grown-up. Now I am, I think. I understand now that marriage means

411

giving as well as taking. I only took from you, Paul. I gave nothing.'

'That isn't true!' Paul said quickly. 'You gave me everything, darling . . . everything you had to give.'

'Except your child!' And as he tried to put a finger across her lips to silence her, Mary said: 'Let me talk about it now, Paul. I want to tell you how awful I felt about it . . . how much I blamed myself for what I did. I thought only of how I could hurt you . . . although I swear to you that I never intended to lose my baby. I just wanted to thwart you over Jackie. It seems so childish now, but it was important to me then. I wanted you to see it *my* way and it seemed you could not. I know now that isn't true . . . that you were acting for my good in forbidding me to push Jackie. I realized it as soon as I lost my baby . . . our baby. But it was too late, then, and I was too proud to admit my mistake. I don't know how you can forgive me, Paul. But I swear to you I'll do everything, anything in the world to make it up to you.'

'Mary, I will not listen to you deriding yourself. I love you, darling, so much that it hurts. These last weeks without you have been unendurable. As if anything could matter any more now I have you back!'

Mary drew a deep breath of sheer contentment. How incredibly lucky she was to be loved by someone like Paul. She didn't deserve it and she knew her own unworthiness. She had broken the first promise she had ever made him . . . that nothing should ever come between them. At the first opportunity, when his wishes had not coincided with hers, she had let her own selfish determination to have her own way at all costs, come near to parting them. And she could never give him back their child.

'Paul, we'll have another baby . . . soon?' she asked tremulously. For perhaps he could forgive and forget if there were another one to take its place.

'Only if you want it,' Paul told her.

'I do! I really do!' Mary said, knowing that it was so.

Paul pulled her tenderly into his arms. As he sat there staring into the glowing fire, he knew himself for the happiest man in the world. Perhaps it was only because he had discovered what it was like to live without her that he had fully understood how much she meant to him ... Mary ... his wife! Maybe all marriages had these moments ... blessed, sacred moments of re-dedication. Maybe it wasn't so easy after all for two people to live in harmony always. But even while they had quarrelled, they had neither ceased to love and he knew now that this would be true of them both all their lives together. Nothing could or would part them for long for they belonged together, each to the other, as he had always known they did. And that love would grow with the years rather than diminish as they found new understanding, learned the art of tolerance and the ways to guard their love.

Mary's thoughts were only of the present and the utter perfection of her welcome home.

THE END